D1576594

Send for the Bad Guy!

A gang of notorious outlaws led by Cain Vender is causing mayhem in Sweetwater County. Their depredations are threatening to overrun the whole of Wyoming. Special agent Drew Henry is reluctant to come out of retirement until he learns that his brother has been killed by the gang. Working undercover as a bar tender, Cole effectively stymied the gang's attempt to rob a bank in a neighbouring county. But he paid the ultimate price for his success. Drew adopts the persona of a deceased train robber to infiltrate the gang. But a conflict of interest in the delectable form of Ruth Vender threatens to overshadow his subterfuge. Will he have the strength of will to carry through the guile needed to defeat the outlaws?

Send for the Bad Guy!

Ethan Flagg

A Black Horse Western
ROBERT HALE

© Ethan Flagg 2016
First published in Great Britain 2016

ISBN 978-0-7198-2013-7

The Crowood Press
The Stable Block
Crowood Lane
Ramsbury
Marlborough
Wiltshire SN8 2HR

www.crowood.com

Robert Hale is an imprint
of The Crowood Press

Typeset by Catherine Williams, Knebworth

Printed and bound in Great Britain by
CPI Group (UK) Ltd, Croydon CR0 4YY

ONE

ON TENTERHOOKS

'They've crossed over Beaver Creek and are heading this way, Marshal.'

The gasped announcement was from Arnold Sawyer. The portly storekeeper had run all the way from the edge of town to deliver the vital news. It was the most exercise he had done in years, and it told. His lungs were pumping hard, the veins on his thick neck sticking out like angry snakes. After delivering the unwelcome news, he slumped onto a bench outside the bank mopping his brow.

Sawyer was the last of a series of lookouts posted at strategic points to signal the approach of the infamous Vender Gang. A secret informant had told the local lawman of the outlaw gang's intention to rob the bank at precisely twelve noon. It was now a quarter hour before the deadline and tensions were running high in the Wyoming town of Lander.

The strained atmosphere was palpable. So heavy you could cut it with a knife. Numerous townsmen had assembled, ready to take up positions facing the entrance to the bank. Indeed, the whole town had been on edge since the news of the expected robbery had been received three days before. Few if any of the citizens had been able to sleep the previous night, such was their heightened state of apprehension.

This was the first time the gang had ventured outside their normal sphere of endeavour. And Marshal Brickfist Ty Fagan fully intended to be the officer who brought the infamous brothers to book. He was a big guy, well able to handle the usual high jinks from cowboys and drunken troublemakers. Even the odd hold-up held no fears for the tough town tamer. But the Vender Gang was a different proposition.

'How many are there?' The lawman's tone was abrupt, a gruffness in tune with the gravity of the situation in which the town now found itself.

'Jackson was holding up six fingers,' came back the wheezing reply.

A nod of accord followed. 'That'll be the four Vender boys and two henchmen,' he added. Only the twitching of Fagan's grey moustache indicated the burden of anxiety he was under. But he was the law in Lander. Maintaining an outwardly composed demeanour was vital to avoid any panic among these homespun townsfolk.

'Remember, boys,' the lawman called out for all to hear. 'No shooting until those guys come out of the bank with the dough. We need to catch them red-handed in the act otherwise they'll wriggle out of any charges brought in a court of law. Guys like these can afford the best lawyers. Crafty dudes whose weasel words can wrap a jury around their little fingers.'

He hawked a glob of spittle into the dust. Brickfist harboured a simmering resentment for defence lawyers. In his experience too many villains had slipped the noose on account of technicalities dug out of the archives by these slippery jaspers.

The half dozen men who had been selected for their shooting prowess were shifting nervously outside the bank awaiting their final instructions. 'OK boys, time to get in position. And make every shot count if'n these guys decide to make a fight of it.'

The sharpshooters quickly dispersed to their allotted hideouts. Two women hurried down the board-walk, quickly disappearing down side streets anxious to reach home and safety before the action started. A boy ran into the street chasing after a ball. He was followed by a frantic mother who dragged the protesting youngster off with some stern words of rebuke.

The storekeeper remained seated. He still had not regained his breath following the spirited dash. Alarm now forced a question that had been bugging him. One that he now posed to the marshal. 'Do you think these Vender boys are planning to take over this county as well as Sweetwater?'

It was a question that had also been bothering the lawman. He squared his broad shoulders, intent on delivering a positive response. 'Not if'n I have any-thing to do with it. All that's needed to come through this safely is for us all to do our bit today.' Fagan then injected a blunt note of grit into the declaration. 'I'm gonna make sure these villains wish they'd never heard of Lander.' He hooked out his pocket watch. Ten minutes to go. 'Now you head off home, Arnold, and make sure that family of your'n keeps their heads down. You've done a good job.'

The praise appeared to lift the storekeeper's spirits. Heaving his bulky frame off the bench, he waddled off across the street to his emporium.

Only Fagan and the bank manager remained.

'You are certain this will work, aren't you Ty?' Hyram Stamp enquired for the fifth time that morning. He was more nervous than a tenderfoot on his first date. 'There's a lot of money sitting in the vault from all the cattle sales we've had recently. And I don't want any of my tellers hurt when those damned Venders start waving their guns around.'

The marshal managed to hold back a caustic retort. He sucked in a deep breath and calmly delivered the same reply uttered previously. 'Just do as the robbers tell you, Hyram. No heroics, no resistance. Comply with their orders and they'll have no reason to hurt anybody. Now get back in there. And don't act so nervous or them critters are bound to smell a rat.'

The manager wiped a handkerchief across his sweat-ing brow. 'This is the first time I've been in the firing line of a bank robbery.' He immediately regretted the unfortunate choice of words. A hand patted his chest. 'And I hope it will be the last. My heart won't stand another day like today.'

'And it will be if'n everybody holds their nerve,' snapped Fagan impatiently. 'Now cool it, mister, and do your job.'

Within minutes Lander's main street was deserted. A lone dog wandered across pausing in the middle to look around. It appeared to sense the heavy air of expectation that gripped the town. Then it spotted a cat on the far side, and the moment passed. A bark of triumph and the hound bolted after its prey. Only the creaking of an ungreased sign swaying in the light breeze disturbed the following silence.

Fluffy puffs of white cloud drifted by overhead. Trees swayed, the rustle of their leaves evoking a tranquil calm that only they felt. And so the town of Lander, population 575 – elevation 7,250 feet, held its collective breath, and waited.

Cain Vender signalled for the gang to haul rein at the bridge spanning Beaver Creek. A sign nailed to the bridge indicated that the turbulent waters marked the county boundary. On this side Sweetwater and safety from capture, on the far side Freemont where the regular law held sway.

Previous forays in search of illicit loot had been to the south-west over the state border with Utah where the law was much more scattered. The terrain was also much more broken making it easier to avoid any pursuit back into Wyoming.

But the word had been passed down the line that the bank in Lander was bursting at the seams with lovely greenbacks. And they were just asking to be picked up by an enterprising bunch of guys like the Venders.

One of the gang, however, voiced his doubts. 'You reckon it's safe venturing into Freemont County, boss?' asked a hard case called Scooter Biggs. 'So far we've stuck to targets in Sweetwater. Any others have been outside Wyoming. Let's hope we ain't bitten off more'n we can chew,' the owlhoot grunted.

'If'n you're getting jittery, Biggs, maybe you should pull out and let real men do the business,' mocked Joey Vender. A tall rangy young tough with a square cut jaw and craggy visage, Joey liked to consider himself a hit with the ladies. His older brothers took great delight in teasing him, but deep down the green-eyed monster was at work.

'I ain't scared,' protested Biggs stiffly. 'Just expressing a need for caution is all.'

'Too much of that dulls a guy's senses, makes him unwilling to take risks,' Cain pontificated. 'In our line of work, danger and playing for high stakes go hand in glove. It's all part of the game.'

'Makes getting up in the morning worthwhile,' interjected Abel Vender. 'None of us wants to work ourselves into an early grave scratching a living on a farm, that's why we rob stagecoaches and banks.'

'And it's time we broadened our horizons closer to

home. That's why we're branching out into Freemont. And if'n this goes well, perty soon the whole county will be under our thumb, just like in Sweetwater.' Cain eyed his associate. 'So are you in or out, Scooter?' The hand resting on his pistol butt was a plain hint as to what the wrong answer would deliver.

The curt response was delivered in a blunt rebuttal of any dissent. Cain Vender was bossing this outfit. Any serious challenge to that authority would be met with a solid and terminal reply. Two months before, Idaho Jack Snapper had made the mistake of posing one too many objections to Cain's way of operating. His body had been tossed into a gorge with three bullet holes in the chest. Only the other Vender brothers were permitted to argue the toss. And they knew when to hold their tongues.

'You don't need to ask that, boss,' replied a chastened Biggs. 'Of course I'm in.' Scooter Biggs was Snapper's replacement. He would need to learn the rules fast if'n he was to continue watching the sun rise.

The outlaw's reply seemed to satisfy Cain. The gang leader was full of confidence regarding their current foray into the neighbouring county. Succeed in Lander and the whole territory would be up for grabs.

'It's gonna be easy as shooting fish in a barrel,' was his considered opinion. The wide mouth broadened into what looked like a smile, although any hint of levity failed to reach his wintry gaze. Where illicit jobs were concerned, his word was raw. Nobody voiced any further dissent.

So far, Cain's tactics had proved to be highly lucrative. Carry on like this and the whole family could retire to a life of luxury in no time. He might even include that turncoat of a brother Samuel.

And that was what he kept telling his sceptical sister when she expressed her disdain for their lawless depredations. Ruth had kept house for her brothers since both their parents had been taken by a virulent attack of cholera. She had struggled hard to remain aloof from the heinous dealings of her siblings. But family loyalty was hard to abandon. With some reluctance Ruth felt she owed her parents a duty of care to at least keep the boys fed and watered. One day perhaps, her persistence might pay off. She lived in hope.

In addition to Ruth, the Vender boys comprised four brothers under the leadership of the eldest, Cain Vender. Next there was Abel, considered at birth to be the one most likely to follow his father into the Church. It was a fatal assumption by the God-fearing preacher. Abel Vender had turned out to be the most bloodthirsty. At least eight killings had been chalked up to his credit by the age of 28.

Esau usually went by the name of Hog on account of his insatiable appetite. He enjoyed nothing more than hunting wild game to provide fresh meat for the pot as a change from the usual stringy rabbits. It was reflected in the guy's corpulent frame. But that didn't prevent him being an adept rifleman. The Sharps Big Fifty was Hog's weapon of choice.

Joey was the youngest. Ruth had striven hard to

steer the boy on to a law-abiding path. But to no effect.
The 21-year-old was hell-bent on following the lead
of his older brothers. A couple of extra dudes, Axell
Robey and Scooter Biggs, added muscle and extra gun
power to their status.

The nonconformist was Samuel. He was the only
Vender brother who had managed to steer clear of
any wrongdoing. Much to the contempt of his other
siblings, Sam had opted to abandon the family home
to run a chicken farm at the bottom end of the
Sweetwater Valley.

Sam was continually pressing Ruth to leave her
no-account kin and go live with him. So far she had
been persuaded to remain at the Vender homestead by
the silky persuasion of brother Cain.

But for how long? It was a source of growing annoyance to the others that would surely reach a climax
sooner rather than later. Sam was increasingly becoming a thorn in the lawless side of the clan. Abel had
even suggested getting rid of the troublesome chicken
shit. However, blood is thicker than water and thus far
the irksome philistine had been reluctantly tolerated.

The family had moved into the territory the previous year following their parents' demise in Omaha,
Nebraska. The Reverend Isaac Vender had been a zeal-
ously ardent firebrand. The older boys had resented
their father's crude attempts to instil his interpreta-
tion of the Good Book's radical philosophy into his
offspring.

The use of a leather belt to encourage conformity

did nothing to further the obsessive reverend's edict. It was merely the catalyst that turned the boys against all forms of established control. A life on the wrong side of the tracks was inevitable. It was perhaps a blessing that Isaac Vender had not lived to witness the slide into lawlessness he had so naively unleashed.

The ranch in the county of Sweetwater, Wyoming, was bought ostensibly to raise cattle. The spread had since proved to be an ideal front to further their iniquitous activities. Prior to their arrival, the notorious Starrbreakers had terrorized Wyoming until their downfall at the hands of a special agent appointed by the Bureau of Advanced Detection. The BAD boy in question was Drew Henry who had successfully infiltrated the gang and put a stop to their felonious activities.

He had since retired from active service with the Bureau and now helped run a spread up country. Rumours abounded that Henry had been in cahoots with the Outlaw Queen, Belle Sherman, who was the real brains behind the Starrbreakers. Although nothing was ever proven, Drew Henry had found it prudent to disappear.[1]

The Venders had shown themselves to be a far more ruthless gang of villains than the Starrbreakers ever were. Sweetwater covered a large area with the existing law widespread and poorly co-ordinated. This assisted

---

[1] Drew Henry's part in the eventual break-up of the Starrbreakers is related in *Outlaw Queen*, also by Ethan Flagg (Black Horse Westerns, Robert Hale, 2011).

the gang's dubious success and was a major factor in prompting Cain to expand his operations beyond.

Most important, however, was the crucial information regarding lucrative jobs supplied by three corrupt law officials based in Rock Springs. Naturally in exchange for a share of the illicit haul. Without their connivance, the Venders would never have got away with so much for so long. As a result they were able to operate with impunity in their own bailiwick. This job in Lander was the first time they had ventured into a neighbouring county. But the expected take was deemed to be worth the risk.

For a full minute, the gang peered across the swirling waters of Beaver Creek. It felt like they were entering a foreign country. Cain sensed the tension among his men and moved to assuage their edginess. 'This is the big one, boys.' Like the marshal down the road apiece, he needed to maintain a gruffly confident persona. 'Pull this off and our reputation will spread like the wind. The name of Vender will be spoken of with awe and respect.' He aimed a poignant look at the two henchmen. 'And that goes for guys that ride with us. Everybody on both sides of law will sit up and take notice, far beyond the limits of Wyoming.'

It was a brief yet poignant speech. And it worked. Drooping shoulders straightened. Money in the pocket was one thing. But a reputation was what all jiggers in their profession craved more than anything. To be somebody so that folks stepped aside when you walked past.

'Let's go,' he said, firmly nudging his cayuse across the bridge. The sound of shod hooves echoed loudly on the wooden slats. On the far side they spurred off along the road to Lander. None of them had spotted any of the concealed sentinels.

On the edge of the town they slowed to a walk. Eyes flicked about, searching for anything that might indicate trouble. Hog was the first to notice that all was not as it should be.

No answer to his grunted concern was forthcoming as the others also began to feel the tension in the air.

'I don't like it,' said Abel, his beady peepers flicking back and forth. 'Something ain't right.'

'You think they might be expecting us?' muttered an unsettled Axell Robey. The gang had slowed up as they neared the middle of town where the bank was located.

His buddy Scooter Biggs added to the growing sense of unease. He spoke out with self-assurance knowing the others were now of a like mind. 'There's nobody around. It feels like the whole town's gone to ground.'

Cain knew he needed to inject a measure of fire into their bellies otherwise this caper was going to crumble before it had even got going. 'You guys are acting like a bunch of old women, frightened of your own shadows. We're going ahead with this job. And anybody who pulls out now ain't more than a cringing whelp.' A bleak eye bore into the hearts of his men, challenging them to complain any further.

The cutting invective aimed at questioning the

men's macho credentials soon stiffened their back-bones. No jasper worth his salt in their world wanted to be regarded as being anything less than a tough hard case.

'We ain't running scared, Cain,' protested Abel, snarling at his brother. 'The boys are just stating the facts. This place ain't normal. I can feel it in my bones.'

'It's just your nerves,' rasped the gang boss. 'Now get a grip and let's get this over with. You all know what to do.' With that he nudged his horse over to the hitching rail opposite the bank.

A myriad eyes peered from numerous crevices, watching as the men went to dismount. The robbers were likewise nervously looking around, still not convinced that everything was hunky dory. The order from Ty Fagan was for the townsfolk to hold their fire until the robbers came out of the bank with the money, when he would challenge them to surrender.

On the veranda outside his quarters above the marshal's office, Fagan was no less edgy than everybody else. He muttered under his breath. 'Come on, you thieving varmints, step down and get inside that bank.' The robbers were hesitating. It was as if they could almost taste the chilling atmosphere. Like his nickname, Brickfist was a man of action. Playing the waiting game was a strain that threatened to wreak havoc with his equilibrium. 'Come on, come on!' he burbled, toying with his rifle.

But frayed nerves were no less thrusting to the fore among his watching sharpshooters. One in particular did not possess the strength of control being exerted by Ty Fagan. Ezra Hackett ran the livery stable. A twitchy jasper at the best of times, he was on the verge of cracking. When it came to competitive shooting, Ezra was in a class of his own. But this was the first time his sights had been aimed at a human target. That was a whole different ball game. His hands were shaking, the trigger finger unsteady and quivering.

It was patently apparent that the unthinkable was about to happen.

TWO

BLACK DAY IN LANDER

A shot rang out, lifting the hat from Axell Robey's head. He was lucky. If Hackett had been more in control and aiming at an inert target, it would have hit home for sure. Suddenly all hell broke loose as every other man took it as a signal to let fly.

Taken completely by surprise, Cain Vender responded in the manner of a true leader by replying calmly and with deliberation. His second bullet took a man down from the veranda on the far side of the street. The victim pitched over the parapet. His body hit the ground with a solid thud that was impossible to ignore. Momentarily stunned, the defenders now realized they were participating in a real fight to the death.

Doc Carter had been standing next to Fagan. The popular medic's sudden death shook the lawman to the core. He quickly dropped to one knee. His plan to outwit the robbers was rapidly falling apart. He volubly

19

cursed the goddamned idiot who had loosed off that shot before the agreed time.

The brief respite gave the invaders a chance to regroup.

It was now patently obvious to Cain that their plans had been known in advance. Somebody had squealed and these townsfolk were ready. Huddled around the entrance to the bank, he brusquely took control. The gang had been in thorny spots before and escaped to tell the tale. He was determined that these durned hayseeds would not get the better of the Vender Gang on this occasion either.

No chance of lifting the dough now. The main thing was to get away unscathed. As he quickly assessed the delicate situation, the question bubbling inside his head was who had dished them to the authorities. The knotty dilemma was tossed aside as the more desperate issue of escape took priority.

Taking cover behind boxes, veranda posts and anything else near at hand, the gang instantly responded with a withering reply backed by Cain's vehement urging. 'Keep their heads down, boys. These critters don't know what they've taken on by resisting the infamous Vender Gang. So let 'em have it!'

It was Marshal Fagan's angry retort at having his perfect ambush prematurely set in motion by some twitchy trigger finger that galvanized the townsmen back into action. Already he was a good man down due to the reckless act. All he could do now was trust that superior firepower would save the day.

'Don't let these skunks get away,' he hollered. 'We've got them penned in and at our mercy. So make every shot count.'

The battle was rejoined in earnest. But Cain Vender had spotted a way out. For all his supposed ingenuity in providing a hot reception, that lunkhead of a tinstar had failed to perceive the obvious. Parked outside the adjacent building to the bank was a high-sided wagon complete with a team of four. The sound of battle was making the horses decidedly restive. Any minute now they could stampede.

'Scooter!' he called to his henchman. 'Up on that wagon pronto and be ready to kick that team into action when I give the word.' Continuing to sling lead out, he called across to Abel. 'You stay with me, brother, and gather the reins of our nags. We're gonna need 'em later. The rest of you get aboard while I keep these guys occupied.'

He tossed the empty revolver aside and drew a second pistol that was stuck in his shellbelt. Blasting away at anything that showed signs of movement in the surrounding buildings on the opposite side of the street, he backed towards the wagon where Abel was tethering the reins.

A cry of pain from one of his men was ignored. The entire focus of his attention was in keeping heads down. In no time the second gun clicked on empty. But by then he was scrambling into the bed of the wagon. 'Whip these critters up, Scooter, and let's get out of here,' he yelled above the ear-splitting cacophony.

The wagon trundled off. Above the riotous tumult, the marshal's dismayed bawling urged the townsmen to greater efforts. After all his careful organization of this ambush, these slimy varmints were about to slip through his fingers.

'Who in thunderation left that wagon there?' he yelled angrily. 'I'll cut his damned heart out.' It was a futile threat that was lost amidst the roar of battle. 'Don't let the scum escape! We had them in the palms of our hands. Chop 'em down!' Tears of frustration welled in his eyes.

Waving hands and stamping feet would do no good, the irate lawman soon realized. He had one last chance to bring any good out of this blundering fiasco. Bending down on one knee to steady his aim, he brought the Winchester to his shoulder. One of the bandits had carelessly stood up to unleash a final flurry of shots.

'Get down, Joey!' brother Abel snapped. 'You'll get your head blown off up there.' But he was too late. The bullet was a foot lower than predicted. Nevertheless it was a fatal hit, striking the kid in the chest. He threw up his arms and tumbled out of the wagon, which was gathering speed.

A rousing burst of approbation erupted from the defenders. 'Well done, Marshal,' came the spirited praise from numerous throats. 'Good shooting, Brick-fist. At least we've gotten one of the bastards.'

Bent low on the front bench, Scooter Biggs hesitated. Should he stop to recover the boy's body?

'Keep going,' Cain ordered. 'Billy's a goner. But we

still have the chance to escape.' More bullets clipped the raised sides of the wagon. But the remaining gang members were well hidden. The good citizens of Lander dispatched a final salvo at the disappearing wagon. Cheers of relief more than anything chased the failed robbers out of the town.

Ty Fagan was more concerned that the varmints did not get away. One townsman had already been killed, and the Venders would slip though his fingers if'n immediate action was not taken. 'You men get your horses,' he called out. 'We need to get after the skunks before they reach the county line.'

Cain Vender was well aware that a posse would be on their trail soon. And they would easily catch up with the wagon. Once they were out of sight, he ordered Biggs to pull up. 'We'll ditch the wagon here. It's too durned slow. Mount up and dig them spurs in.'

The gang needed no second bidding. Already they could hear the pounding of hoof beats to their rear. Moments later the posse with Ty Fagan in the lead came dashing around a bend a hundred yards back. On spotting the fleeing villains, some of the posse members let fly with their handguns, more from the adrenaline-pumping exhilaration of the chase than any hope of making a hit at that range.

'Save your bullets, boys,' advised Fagan. 'Concentrate on stretching the legs of your nags. It's only a couple more miles to the bridge.'

Heads lowered, the wind flattening the brims of their hats, the pursuers urged their mounts onward.

But nothing was going to stop Cain Vender and his men from reaching the sanctuary of Sweetwater County. Whooping and hollering, hats waving, Robey and Biggs were the first to clatter over the wooden bridge. Much to Cain's annoyance, they were acting as if they had succeeded in their mission. In reality, they were empty-handed and one man down.

'Cut the yammering, you turkeys,' rasped Cain dragging his horse to a halt once they were safely across Beaver Creek. 'This ain't no cause for celebration.'

He needed to be certain that the posse would not follow. A regular marshal's jurisdiction ended at the county line. And Ty Fagan was no different. The lawman signalled a halt on the Freemont side of the border.

'Ain't we going after them, Marshal?' enquired one eager posse man.

'We couldn't even if'n I was allowed to and they know it,' replied the morose starpacker. 'My hands are tied. Those Venders have the authorities eating out of their hands over yonder. The way things stand in Sweetwater at the present, we haven't a snowball's chance in hell of getting a conviction.'

Watching the stymied posse fuming on the far side of the bridge stimulated Axell Robey to call out a mocking epithet.

'Shut up your darned mouth, Robey,' snapped Cain. 'That tin star is likely to throw caution to the wind if'n you start bugging him. Now let's ride. There's some serious questions to be asked if'n we're gonna find out who shopped us.'

THREE

FALSE ACCUSATION

It was over supper a couple of days later that the discussion became heated. Speculation had been rife as to who had spilled the beans regarding the failed robbery. Threats as to what would happen to the perpetrator were tossed out in wild abandon. But without a name the threats were as impotent as a barren cow. The culprit was still a complete mystery by the time Ruth was pouring the coffee.

A knock on the door terminated the endlessly futile debate. Ruth answered it. A smile graced her serene face. In her eyes their law-abiding brother Samuel was always welcome at the family homestead.

The arrival of the so-called pariah was received with scornful leers by the others. Sam ignored the less than cordial reception.

'I heard about Joey,' the visitor declared, expressing his deepest regret at the boy's shooting. But any heart-felt commiserations were tainted with a vindic-tive asperity as the guy's hard features clouded over. 'It would never have happened if'n you turkeys had kept the kid out of your half-baked schemes. His head was swayed by empty promises of fame and fortune. It's your damned fault he's dead.'

Abel leapt to his feet. 'So now we know who shopped us to the law,' he spat out while grabbing a knife off the table. 'It was you who gave the game away, wasn't it? I allus knew you were a yellow snake, Sam. Nobody can get any lower than playing the Judas against his own kin.' The knife arm swung back to deliver his own lethal verdict on the indictment. 'There's only one answer to a vile stunt like that.'

Only the quick-witted interception of Cain pre-vented yet another fatal blunder. 'There'll be no vigilante reprisals in this house. One brother is already dead. And taking the law into your own hands won't get us anywhere.' He forced Abel to drop the knife then pushed him back into his chair. 'Now give the guy a chance to speak. OK then, Sam. What have you gotten to say about this?'

Cain's thoughts had sadly been running along similar lines to those of Abel.

Samuel Vender was the eldest of the clan by a year. His thick curly hair stuck out from beneath a battered felt hat. In the last year too much grey had infiltrated the Vender brown, becoming the dominant hue. Deeply furrowed lines creased a jaded countenance. All instigated by his rift with the family, they made him look ten years older than his thirty-six years.

It had not been easy sticking with the upright respectability fostered by his parents. Regular readings from the Good Book helped maintain his stance, but the constant friction with his younger brothers had worn him down.

And there did not appear to be any end in sight, except for a Boot Hill grave with the name Vender carved on the tombstone. Joey Vender was only the first. The way things were going, he would not be the last. His only consolation was that Ruth always offered her support.

She stepped in now to admonish the vindictive Abel. 'You should be ashamed of yourself,' she scolded, jabbing a finger into the guy's chest. 'Sam would never reveal your underhanded dealings to anybody. To even consider such a thing is above contempt.'

Abel scoffed. 'Letting a woman argue your case is just like you, Judas.'

The older brother had heard enough. He stepped forward and grabbed Abel by the scruff of the neck, hauling him upright. Inches apart, he delivered his own scathing rebuke. 'Don't you ever accuse me of putting young Joey's life in the firing line. I couldn't give a toss if'n you bunch of critters get your heads blown off. But it won't be on account of me ratting on blood kin. I have more pride than to lower myself to your level.' He threw Abel aside like an old sock, deliberately turning his back on the man who moments before had been prepared to stick a knife in him.

Abel merely sneered, but made no move to expand on his allegations.

Hog went on shovelling his supper down a welcoming gullet. Even though he was taking in all that was being said, there was very little that could prevent Hog from enjoying his food. And Sister Ruth certainly knew her way around a kitchen. Of that there could be no disagreement amongst any of them.

'I don't know why you stay with these useless no-goods,' Sam said to his sister. 'The offer to stay with me still stands.'

'You know I could never leave here. It's my home. And I hate to think what would become of these guys if'n I left.' She threw a disparaging look at the three outlaws. 'At least while I'm around, there's a chance I can convince them to go straight. Ma and Pa would have expected nothing less of me.'

'Be it on your head Ruth,' scoffed Sam. 'I ain't gotten your optimistic outlook. All I see for these jaspers at the end of the trail is a chunk of hot lead, or a hangman's noose. Not much of a choice, is it?' His voice softened, assuming a degree of contrition at odds with his previous anger. 'The folks in Lander know that I'm separate from you boys. So they'll raise no objection to me picking up Joey's body.'

The heated tension of moments before quickly dissolved, being replaced by one of sorrow. Even Hog was momentarily distracted from his favourite pastime. He voiced the torment they were all feeling. 'Guess we'll have to make our own little cemetery with a headstone surrounded by a white picket fence.' A respectful silence enveloped those left behind. 'That spot out back of the house over by the cottonwoods is a good place, don't you think?'

Four heads offered forlorn nods of agreement. Sam Vender bade them a desultory farewell and left to carry out his grim duty. There were no cheery goodbyes. The resentment of their eldest brother's choice of lifestyle remained a point of controversy. But for the moment, at least until after the funeral, a certain brief harmony would exist between them.

It wasn't long before the conversation once again reverted to a heated discussion as to who had actually shopped them.

Ruth and Hog were the first to retire with the question still hanging in the air. They were soon followed by Robey and Biggs, who ambled across to the barn. Their quarters were located in a room above the stable. The ever-present smell of horse dung was a fact of life they had gotten used to. Certainly not the comfortable surroundings occupied by the Venders, the barn was more than adequate for two itinerant drifters.

This was the first time either man could claim to have a place of his own. Three meals and all found was not to be sniffed at. Not to mention pay days that could be extremely lucrative. It beat punching cows for a living and having to share a bunkhouse with a dozen other rannigans.

Back in the parlour, Abel sat brooding over by the grate, staring into the flickering embers while nursing his hurt pride, and a glass of moonshine. Cain decided to give his brother some space and ambled outside to clear his head with a smoke. There was much to think on before he could consider putting his head down.

A quarter hour later, Scooter Biggs emerged from the barn. The night was calm. The canopy of black sprinkled with a myriad twinklers implied a peaceful haven. A stark contrast to the simmering tensions of the ranch's human occupants. Biggs paused in the doorway, unsure of his next move. There were things on his mind that needed clearing. Tentatively he approached Cain with the intention of relating what had transpired in Rock Springs the previous weekend.

Quick on the uptake, Cain sensed that his associate's presence was for no idle chinwag. The guy's nervous hesitation gave him away. Cain knew that something was bugging his associate. 'You got some kinda beef, Scooter, then spit out,' came the brisk command. Following the confrontation with Sam, he was in no mood for trivialities.

'I don't want to be a squealer, boss, but... ' Still he wavered. The gunman was shuffling his feet like a kid caught with his fingers in the cookie jar. Cain's glowering regard was intimidating and made him question the decision to open up. 'Maybe I'm speaking out of turn.'

But it was too late for second thoughts now. He was past the point of no return. Cain knew there was an issue at stake and he was not about to have it pushed aside. 'You best tell me now. I ain't in the mood for no shilly-shallying. So out with it.' A blunt-eyed stare drilled into the hovering outlaw.

'Well … I was with Abel last Saturday in the Big Horn. We had been drinking with some of the Saratoga crew.' Cain was instantly all ears. Biggs then went on to explain how Abel couldn't keep his mouth shut. 'I tried to pull him aside, but he was so keyed up about the coming raid. Nothing was going to stop him bragging about it. He must have reckoned to be on safe ground in the Big Horn. Those Saratoga boys are no angels themselves.'

Once the revelation had been exposed, Cain nodded. His face assumed a vindictive grimace. 'You done the right thing in telling me, Scooter.' The henchman breathed out a sigh of relief. Cain then slammed a bunched fist into the door jamb. 'That idiot will be the death of us. He needs a good shaking down. And I'm the guy to do it.'

'You won't mention it was me that spilt the beans, will you?' Biggs appealed.

'Don't worry yourself on that score,' Cain assured his associate. 'I know how to handle that blabbermouth.'

There had been half a dozen of Abel's cronies in the Big Horn that night so there was no cause for the culprit to suspect one of his own men. Having revealed his suspicions, Biggs returned to the barn. Cain remained out front drawing hard on a stogie, his anger intensifying by the second. Finally tossing the butt aside, he stumped back into the parlour to confront his brother.

Without any preamble, he slung out an accusatory finger. 'I've been thinking hard about this turncoat. And I reckon it was you who snitched about the raid when you went into Rock Springs last Saturday. You were drunk as a skunk when you got home. Showing off I'll bet to your buddies.'

Abel spluttered and blustered, trying to refute what was now patently obvious. But his denials lacked any conviction. He had no choice but to admit his blunder.

'That was a damn fool thing to do. A blunder that led to the death of our kid brother,' rasped Cain, his blotchy face livid with anger. 'I'm never going to forgive you for that. The only thing in your favour is that it was the drink talking. You never could hold your liquor. So it wasn't deliberate on your part. But you'll have to live with what you've caused 'til your dying day.'

The normally granite hard exterior wilted under the scornful denunciation. 'Gee, Cain, ever since I realized what I'd done, it's been eating me up inside. It was a stupid thing to do. I know that now. You're right. The drink got the better of me. I couldn't resist swanking about the job.' His head slumped in shame.

Cain knew that his brother was genuinely full of remorse. He didn't need to say anything more. The two brothers sat opposite one another, each wrapped in his own morose cogitations. It was Cain who finally broke the silence. And that was to determine the principle issue at stake. 'No sense now in crying over spilt milk. The main thing is to find out who was listening in and told the authorities. It looks mighty like we have an informer in our midst.'

'The skunk must have been planted in Rock Springs by the BAD organization. They set up an office in Laramie after taking out the Starrbreakers a couple of years back,' Abel stuttered out, trying desperately to redeem himself. 'Our other heists must have spooked them. I was among friends in the Big Horn. None of those boys would have shopped us.'

'All we have to do now is find out who it is then. You tell me that and I might cut you some slack.' But all Abel could do was offer a pathetic shrug of ignorance.

FOUR

EXPOSURE

The three brothers were up late the next morning. Too much moonshine had been consumed the night before, especially by Abel who hoped that his foolhardy outburst would have gone away. All he brought downstairs with him was a thick head. His elder brother's glowering welcome did nothing to allay his fears.

Hog was already at the table enjoying a plate of bacon and eggs along with the two henchmen. Biggs eyed Abel Vender nervously when he made his appearance. But the loose-lipped jasper displayed no sign that he harboured any evil intentions. Cain had clearly persuaded him that his suspicions had not come from inside the gang.

The meal was consumed in silence. Ruth made no effort to lighten the mood of melancholia as she topped up their coffee mugs. It was Cain who finally cut through the tense atmosphere.

'You boys practise some shooting out back,' he instructed his newest recruits. 'I reckon you need it after yesterday's failure. I'm going into Rock Springs to see if'n I can suss out the snake who wrecked our plans.'

Robey felt irked at having his gunslinging prowess brought into question. The more feisty of the two, he was all set to blurt out his objections to such an insult. His buddy quickly butted in to smooth things over. 'Sure thing, boss. Guess it won't do us any harm to boost our gunplay. Let's hope you have some success in town.'

'I'll come with you,' suggested Abel, lumbering to his feet. 'I could do with a visit to town.'

'After what you've done? Forget it, buster.' Cain's anger at his brother was biting and pulled no punches. If'n the clown thought a night's sleep would settle matters he was sadly mistaken. It would be some time before their familial bond, fractious at the best of times, would return to an even keel. 'I don't want you anywhere near a saloon after that big mouth of your'n caused this mess. There's plenty of work needs doing on the ranch to keep you busy while I'm away. And keep off the moonshine! You see that he walks a straight line, sis.'

'Don't worry. I'll keep an eye on him,' concurred an equally starchy Ruth Vender. 'There are enough jobs in the house to keep him out of trouble for a month of Saturdays.'

Abel Vender scowled. But he had no choice but to accept the chastisement.

The hired help struggled to keep their faces straight as they left the house. They sauntered back to the barn to collect their guns and set up some empty cans for target practice. That was when Scooter decided to apprise his buddy of the previous night's conversation with Cain Vender. 'Thought it best to tell you that I spilled the beans about Abel shooting off his mouth in the Big Horn.'

Robey was stunned. 'What?' he hollered out. 'Man, that was a darned foolish thing to do. He's touchy at the best of times. The guy will skin you alive if'n he finds out.'

'I couldn't let it go unchallenged once young Joey had been killed. It was Abel's damned fault,' Biggs declared, vehemently defending his actions. 'And when he made no attempt to admit he was in the wrong, that was the last straw. Maybe even then I'd have kept quiet. But a guy who purposely tries to shift the blame on to his own brother, and then tries to stick a knife in him. That was one step too far.'

'You sure Abel won't learn the truth?' Robey persisted. 'You're walking a tightrope here, buddy.'

'Don't reckon so. Cain seems to have talked him round. So I'm in the clear.'

With that settled, they proceeded to outdraw each other against the static targets.

When Cain arrived in Rock Springs, he went directly to the courthouse where he was sure his underhanded associates would be ensconced. Without knocking he barged straight in. And sure enough, the three conniving officials were discussing the failure of the Lander bank job.

Judge Gideon Fitzroy was the first to speak. He was a corpulent, rather untidy jasper, and by far the oldest of the trio. An unlit cigar was stuck in his mouth. The legal credentials he often bragged about were more the result of wheeler-dealing and backhanders than through any comprehension of legal procedures. A perpetual air of suspicion registered on a blotched face made ruddy by too much whiskey. His grating reaction to the outlaw's sudden entry confirmed his penchant for the demon drink.

'We were wondering when you'd show your face. What in tarnation happened the other day?' He swung to face the newcomer. Thumbs tucked into a sweat-stained silk vest implied a demand for answers.

'That raid would have been our biggest take so far. It would have seen us all set up for a long time to come,' grumbled the legal prosecutor. Elmer Hyde was a tall, austere individual, dressed in black like an undertaker. A suitably dour regard usually reserved for intimidating courtroom witnesses confronted the newcomer. 'I needed my cut to pay off some outstanding debts. That Arab stallion I had brought in from Cheyenne didn't come cheap.' He was hoping the blustering effect would intimidate the infamous outlaw.

Much to his disappointment, Cain Vender was not in the least overawed by these charlatans. 'Quit your griping,' he snapped out. 'They were waiting for us. We were betrayed. You think I want to be burying my kid brother?'

The surly glower soon shut the prosecutor's mouth. Cain wasn't about to take any shit from these dudes. Indeed, he harboured nothing but contempt for their kind. He and his gang openly accepted their way of life. But this set of devious jaspers skulked in the shadows. Outwardly trying to convey an air of respectability, they were secretly creaming off the town's revenue from their illicit skulduggery. If'n the local populace ever discovered how they managed to inhabit those swanky houses on the edge of town, there would be a riot.

That said, the gang needed such denizens in order to operate in a free and easy manner. The county officials could manipulate the law. More importantly, they had access to information pointing to the best jobs, while he and his boys provided the muscle to carry them off successfully. All that had suddenly come tumbling down in Lander. And these guys wanted answers that he did not possess.

Cain was as mystified as anybody at the cause of the ambush. And no less angry. 'Somebody must have grassed us up to the law in Freemont County,' he offered somewhat lamely. 'There isn't no other way they could have been so well prepared for us coming.'

'What about that chicken-rearing brother of your'n?' asked the third man, Sheriff Tash Speakman. 'He's known to be against what you boys are doing. Maybe he's had enough of being branded with your mark and decided to get even.'

Cain's scathing grimace pierced the tactless skin of the bent lawman. He took a step forward, forcing the man on to the back foot. 'My brother would never drop his own kind into the dung heap. And anybody who suggests otherwise will find himself answering to me.' His hand rested on the butt of his revolver.

Judge Fitzroy held up his hands. 'All right, easy there, Cain,' he appeased the outlaw. 'Tash was only trying to eliminate people from being on the list of suspects. We know Sam is an all right guy. And we know all the other folks in town as well.'

'I can't think of anybody round here. This guy must be in the pay of the Bureau of Advanced Detection.' The prosecutor scratched his thatch of wavy black hair. 'But any BAD guy working in this area would have surely reported in to us. Ain't that right, Gideon?'

'Not if'n they suspected the robberies we've been arranging for Cain and his boys were insider jobs,' countered the wily judge. 'They'd have kept it quiet.'

'You think we're under suspicion?' iterated an alarmed Sheriff Speakman. 'We've always taken the utmost care to keep our involvement a secret.' There was no answer to that dilemma.

'Are there any new guys in town?' asked Cain. 'Somebody has to be passing the word. So it stands to reason that he must be an outsider.'

The three officials stroked their chins while considering the suggestion.

'Only one I can think of is Cole Henry, the bartender at the Big Horn,' said Speakman. 'He's only been working there a couple of months.'

'Could be our man,' enthused an upbeat Judge Fitzroy. 'But how are we going to winkle him out? He sure ain't gonna volunteer his true colours. It needs guile and cunning to flush a bastard like that out of the woodwork.'

'And I reckon I know just how to do it,' preened Cain. The cold gleam in his eye matched the cynical hint of a smile.

The following day, Axell Robey was installed at the bar of the saloon. He was nursing a beer and minding his own business when a staggering Abel Vender wandered in. Robey had not been present when Abel had made his blundering announcement. So the barman had no reason to harbour any suspicions.

Henry eyed the newcomer. The guy had clearly been at the hooch in other saloons before he arrived at the Big Horn. Abel crossed to the bar and ordered a whiskey, purposefully avoiding any eye contact with his sidekick. He was grumbling and grousing to himself as he sipped the drink.

'Something bothering you, Abel?' asked the bartender. 'You seem a bit down in the mouth today.'

'And so I should be.' The outlaw's slurred reply was accompanied by another slurp, half of which dribbled down his chin, disappearing into his beard. 'It was my durned fault that poor Joey was shot dead in Lander. I opened fire too soon and bought the kid a plot in the cemetery.'

More mutterings full of regret at his rash action found the barman listening in with suppressed eagerness as Abel summoned him to come closer. The outlaw peered around anxious that nobody else should overhear what he had to say. 'But I'm gonna make it up to the kid so he won't have died in vain.' His next maudlin remark was barely above a whisper. Cole Henry was all ears. 'On Friday we're going back to Lander. And this time I won't screw up. We'll get that dough. And nobody's gonna stop us this time.' He wagged a finger under the barman's nose then tossed the rest of his drink down and staggered over to a chair. And there the soused owlhooter slumped over, ostensibly out for the count.

Henry waited a few minutes to ensure the alleged drunk was asleep before calling across to a colleague that he had to go out for a spell. Removing his apron, Henry slipped out the back door. At the same time, Robey also left by the front door and watched to see where Henry went.

Moments later the barman emerged from a side road and spurred off out of town. Robey followed behind, making doubly certain to keep his distance. The last thing he needed was to be spotted. He followed the guy into the hills along an old deer track until Henry finally stopped by a hollow stump of a tree. After scribbling on a piece of paper, he dropped the note into the opening.

A quick look around to ensure he was alone, then he retraced his steps. Robey was well concealed in a cluster of boulders as the rider passed him by. Once Henry was out of sight, Robey retrieved the note and spurred off at a gallop back to the Vender place where the others were eagerly awaiting his report.

'How did it go?' enquired a brisk and eminently sober Abel Vender. 'Did the rat fall into the trap?'

'He left this in a tree,' replied Robey, handing over the note. 'I ain't read it. But I'm guessing it ain't for a meeting with a lady friend.'

'Hand it over!' rapped Cain, snatching the missive from the outlaw's hand. After scanning the contents, his brow furrowed into thick worms of fury.

'So what does it say?' rasped Abel. 'Is he the turn-coat?' Cain handed the note across. His brother read it aloud in a rasping snarl. *Venders planning another raid on Lander bank this Friday.*

An angry rumble of discord filled the ranch house parlour. So they had been right.

'The rat must have an accomplice close by who visits that hollow tree regularly,' declared Cain.

'Now we know the identity of that snake in the grass, what we gonna do about it?' posed Scooter Biggs.

'Make darned sure he don't shop us again.'

'You mean…?'

'That's right,' Cain interjected acidly. 'We rub the skunk out permanently. And we do it so's those BAD guys are left in no doubt what happens when they go up against the Venders.'

'But won't they just send in another agent?' objected Hog, stuffing another corn dog into his mouth.

'Then we'll get rid of him as well,' snapped Abel. 'Nobody is going to put the hobbles on what we have going here, boys. There's too much to lose.'

'So what's your plan, boss?' asked an eager Axell Robey.

'We'll wait until the Big Horn closes tonight and Henry returns to that cabin he's occupying in Pathfinder Draw.' An ugly leer crossed the gang leader's hard face. 'Then we let the world know what happens to informers in Sweetwater County. Those federal guys might have broke up the Starrbreakers. But they're gonna find the Venders are a whole different proposition.'

FIVE

A MESSAGE FROM LARAMIE

Drew Henry was repairing a fence over on the north quarter when he noticed the plume of dust rising above a low knoll. It must be somebody coming from the ranch, he surmised. He swilled his mouth out with tepid water before spitting it out. A dirty bandanna stroked the sweat from his face and neck as he waited to see who was paying him a call in the middle of the day. Perhaps Frank had sent Lee Fu, the Chinese cook, with his midday vittles.

One thing was for darned sure. It would not be Gabby.

Drew had been instrumental in saving the Circle K ranch from the heinous Starrbreakers two years before. Following the break-up of the gang, Gabby's brother Frank Kendrick had taken Drew on as an equal partner in the Circle K spread. The death of

Leroy Starr was a milestone in recent history, marking the end of Wyoming's most lawless period.

As a federal agent with the Bureau of Advanced Detection, Drew had infiltrated the gang to gain their confidence and so bring them to justice. But it was a brutal and hard-won battle that had taken a lot out of him. In view of an ever-growing closeness to Gabby Kendrick, the one-time agent decided to tender his resignation. He wanted nothing more to do with hunting down brigands and riff-raff. Ranching offered a far more peaceful life, free from the ever-present danger of a bullet in the back.

Following an obligatory spell of courtship, Drew and his one true love were married in Casper. Their fervent hope was, like the fairy tales of his youth had promised, to live happily ever after. And so it could have been, had not Gabby been struck down by a virulent attack of the fever. They say time is a great healer. Drew was not convinced. It would take a sackful of sunsets to ease the pain of her loss.

He still felt that heart-rending ache in his chest. As bad now as the day she passed away, clutched in his arms. Tears ran down his stubble-coated cheeks as the heart-rending memories were rekindled. Hard work was the only cure to keep his mind from dwelling on what might have been.

Frank had tried his best to lighten the mood of despair. After all, he had lost a much-loved sister. But without Gabby's effervescent spirit, the ranch in Drew's eyes had lost that special quality of magic.

The rider appeared on the crest of the knoll. Drew's eyes screwed up, focussing on the blue uniform redolent of the US Postal Service. The guy came to a shuddering halt close to where Drew had stopped work. He sure was in a hurry.

'Are you Drew Henry?' he asked.

'That's me,' came back the brisk reply.

'Have you any form of identification? This is a special delivery from Laramie that requires a signature.' The mailman held an official envelope in his hand. But he had no intention of passing it over until the recipient's credentials had been verified.

Drew's eyes narrowed. His back stiffened. Laramie! It could only be from one source. The BAD organization. Fishing out a bill of sale from his vest pocket for some barbed wire, he handed it over. The man studied the name thereon and receipt signature. Only then was he prepared to release the missive.

After signing for it, the man tipped his hat and departed, leaving Drew staring hard at the buff-coloured envelope sporting its unique emblem of an eagle perched on two crossed revolvers. Even before he read the contents, he knew what lay therein. He slowly slit open the cover and removed the single sheet of typed paper.

It was brief and direct:

FOR THE ATTENTION OF DREW HENRY, YOUR EXPERTISE NEEDED URGENTLY. PLEASE REPORT TO THE BAD OFFICE IN LARAMIE AS SOON AS POSSIBLE.

And it was signed by Drew's old boss:

Isaac Thruxton.
P.S. BRING YOUR GUNS.

A federal warrant was included to cover the rail fare.

Drew read the missive again. No detail, no intimation as to what his old boss wanted. Just a summons to head for Laramie immediately. The ex-BAD boy smiled to himself. 'Just like you, Colonel,' he muttered under his breath. 'Expect a guy to down tools and jump to your bidding.'

His initial reaction was to screw up the letter and toss it aside. He was retired from the kind of work Colonel Thruxton would expect from him. Yet deep down, an old yearning stirred his bones. The adrenaline-pumping excitement of the chase, the final running to ground of wrongdoers. It was a feeling that never went away. Had Gabby still been in the frame, he would have had no reason to resume his old life.

Rheumy eyes misted over. All he had left now were blissful memories that would be with him until he made that last round-up and joined her. But that's all they were, memories. Life on this earth still had to go on. And ranching was becoming a chore that had lost its appeal.

Drew felt a tingle of anticipation coursing through his body. That old exhilaration of pitting your wits against a ruthless foe. Once a guy had earned his spurs, he never quite abandoned the thrill of the hunt culminating in the satisfaction of being a part of seeing justice administered.

He quickly finished mending the fence then returned to the ranch house. His first job was to go up to his room, their room. All of Gabby's effects had been left as they were. Perhaps now was the time to pack them away. That could be done later. Gleaming eyes strayed to the locked chest, which he now opened for the first time since that fateful day after he had gunned down Leroy Starr. Had Gabby still been a tangible part of his life rather than merely a spiritual presence, he would never have considered his next move.

Gingerly, he took out the tooled shellbelt complete with holstered Colt Peacemaker. He lifted out the heavy revolver. It felt good, fitting his hand like a glove. The touch of the cold, hard metal sent a shiver of expectancy racing through his taut frame. The days, months and years slipped away. He strapped the belt around his lean hips. Fingers flexed in anticipation. Then he drew the weapon and twirled it on his middle finger, flipping it up into the air before slotting it back into the holster.

Lips pulled apart revealing a toothy smile. He still had the knack.

Drew Henry was back in business.

Two days were needed to sort out his affairs. After Frank Kendrick had read the letter he understood his partner's need to leave. 'Whatever this business entails, you make sure to come back safe and well. There'll always be a place for you on the Circle K.' The two friends shook hands. Before he left the ranch, Drew paid a visit to the grave of his beloved Gabby. Tears welled in his eyes when he finally managed to drag himself away.

Drew arrived in Laramie the following day. He headed straight to the office that he knew so well on Alabany Street. A shock was in store for the retired detective when he knocked on the door of the BAD Agency. The man who greeted him was a shadow of his former self.

The iron-grey hair was now almost white. No longer the stalwart Union cavalry officer who had been decorated for bravery in the war, Isaac Thruxton exuded an impression of haunted despair. His handshake remained firm, the welcome for his best agent genuine and sincere.

'It's good to see you again, Drew,' he said, forcing a smile on to his drawn face. Yet the air of cheeriness never quite reached the colonel's blue eyes. 'I know it must have been a tough decision for you to come here.' He ushered the newcomer into his office. 'But you're the only guy who can undertake this particular job.'

The two men were as different in appearance as chalk and cheese. The tall buckskin-clad visitor with his Texan drawl towered over the diminutive boss of the BAD organization who sported a tailor-made blue suit over a crisp white shirt. Polished handmade tan boots completed the regalia of a successful man.

'The Agency must be doing well,' was Drew's comment as he cast a measured eye over his old boss. His probing gaze then shifted to the photographs of other BAD agents lining the office walls. Some with black ribbons surrounding the frames had died in the line of duty. 'Whatever this job involves,' he remarked pointing to the array of active agents, 'it seems to me that you already have enough guys available.' A critical eye swung towards his boss. 'So why me? Ain't you forgotten that I have retired from this game?'

Thruxton coughed to hide his uneasiness. A tightness around the eyes revealed a degree of tension above and beyond what could normally be expected. He moved round his desk and slumped into his chair. The broad shoulders drooped, as if they were carrying the weight of the world. Drew couldn't fail to heed the distinct air of melancholia surrounding the legendary leader of the BAD organization.

A frown creased his tanned face. There was more to this than just another job. What was bugging the colonel? The guy refused to meet his gaze. 'There's something you ain't telling me, Colonel. And I'm not just talking about the urgency of the job you called on me to undertake.'

He waited while the hunched figure lit up a cigar. A delaying tactic that saw him drawing hard on the Havana Special. Only then did the grim truth come pouring forth. 'You're right, of course. This is no ordinary task. But you are the only man who can undertake it.' Again he paused, drawing on the cigar. The apprehension pulsated from every pore of his being.

Drew himself was becoming increasingly disturbed. 'Come on!' he almost shouted. 'Out with it. What's so all-fired different about this particular job?'

Thruxton sucked in a deep lungful of air. 'It's your brother Cole ... I sent him up to Rock Springs in Sweetwater County to gather information on the Vender Gang so's we could put them away.' He swallowed. 'He was killed last week trying to pass vital details over to one of our men.'

Drew's mouth fell open. The blood drained from his face as he turned away to hide his anguish. Cole dead? It didn't seem possible. Only a couple of weeks back he had received a letter from his brother. The kid had seemed fine and dandy then. A suggestion to meet up had been proposed. No reply had as yet been sent. Now it never would be.

This job Cole had been undertaking must have been in full swing at the same time. Secrecy was a firm policy of the organization when an agent was in the field. So it was understandable that no hint had been proffered. For a long minute, silence engulfed the two associates.

It was Drew who asked for details relating to the grim tidings. His voice crackled with emotion. 'So what information do we have to go on?' he muttered, ashen-faced.

Without speaking, Thruxton produced a newspaper and handed it to the agent. It was the *Wyoming Sentinel* dated the previous week. The headline leapt off the front page and grabbed him by the throat – SECRET AGENT FOUND HANGING IN BARN. The report went on to describe the events that had led to the discovery of the body.

When Cole Henry had failed to turn up for work, his boss, the owner of the Big Horn saloon in Rock Springs, had ridden over to his cabin to investigate. Craig Wesscott had discovered the body with a note pinned to it, which read – *This is what happens to informers in Sweetwater County.* It was not signed. But it was patently obvious that the Venders were to blame.

The reporter sent to investigate the murder had learned that Cole Henry was an undercover agent working for the BAD organization based in Laramie. He had been sent to trap the infamous Vender Gang and bring them to justice. The initial attempt to ensnare the gang in the adjacent county had failed. Another alleged robbery at the same place in Lander had been a hoax to expose the informer in their midst.

Clearly the gang had discovered his identity and decided to make an example of the unfortunate victim. Cole Henry paid the ultimate price for his selfless act of bravery.

'You did right to call me back in, Colonel.' Drew's response was delivered in a flat monotone, his features remained hard and disturbingly cold. Yet inside he was a seething mass of tangled nerve endings. 'Nobody else could take on this job. All I have to do now is figure out my strategy to net the skunks.'

Now that the worst part of the interview was over, Isaac Thruxton was once more able to assume his normally efficient persona. 'I've been giving that some serious consideration,' he said, gesturing for Drew to take a seat. 'You were successful in infiltrating the Starrbreakers up in the Hole-in-the-Wall country by adopting an alias. As we both know, that almost came to grief when Beavertail Bob Luman escaped from the Pen. I think you should adopt the same guise with the Venders. But this time we'll make certain that nobody turns up to blow your cover.'

'I'm thinking that you already have somebody in mind.'

'You know me, Drew.' The Agency chief's craggy façade broke into a half smile. This time it was far more relaxed. Grief still hovered over the two men, but it was no longer devoid of purpose. A ploy was being put forward to bring justice for the injured party as well as maintaining law and order in the territory of Wyoming. 'And you also know the aspirations of the Agency.'

'We never give up,' quoted Drew, casting a mordant eye towards the BAD insignia and its slogan on the back wall of the office. His voice measurably toughened. 'And there's no way I will abandon the hunt until every last one of you Venders are pushing up the daisies or dangling from a rope's end.' The softly spoken vow of revenge was a promise for his brother as much as for the organization. 'So have you figured out how we're going to put words into action, boss?'

'I have indeed, Drew my boy.' Thruxton's positive reaction stirred the newly installed BAD agent. 'Once you leave this room, Drew Henry will once again settle into retirement. He will be resurrected as a bank robber with the colourful handle of Cracker Dan Spurlock.'

The unusual soubriquet produced a quizzical comeback. 'Can't say that I've heard of the guy. But a jasper boasting a crazy name like that has to have a history.'

'He was an expert in opening safes using dynamite. His penchant was for train robberies.' The chief held up a hand to allay any fears. 'And before you ask, the guy died last month in the territorial prison at Santa Fe. He came off worst in a knife fight. A fellow prisoner took exception to having his tobacco ration misappropriated. The Cracker's misfortune is going to be your ticket of access into the Vender Gang.'

A cynical regard followed the chief's assertion. 'I hope you're right, boss. I sure wouldn't want this guy turning up out of the blue like Beavertail Bob did.'

Thruxton shook his head. 'No chance of that. One of our men down there checked the grave marker personally and sent me a cable. He's dead all right. And he never operated north of the New Mexico line. So the chances of the Venders being acquainted with the guy are exceedingly slim. They might well have heard the name. But that's all. It's your call how you portray him.' He handed Drew a cigar and poured them both a slug of finest Scotch whisky. 'A toast to the successful elimination of the Vender Gang.' They both raised their glasses. 'One important thing Cole found out before he died was that the gang could not have pulled off their heists without inside help.'

'What are you trying to say, boss?'

'He reckoned there must be some corrupt officials feeding the gang information in return for a cut of the proceeds. Treacherous scorpions like that are as bad if not worse than the actual hit men.' Thruxton paused to allow the import of his revelation to sink in. 'They are the ones you'll need to convince if'n you're going to be accepted into the gang.'

The two men drank slowly. There was much to think about. The Scotch slid down a treat, forming a warm glow in the pit of Drew Henry's stomach. He then made a silent promise to the spirit of his brother. *Here's to you, Cole. I'll make darned certain your death was not in vain.*

'So how is Cracker Dan Spurlock going to pull this off?' the revitalized outlaw asked. Now that the preliminaries were over, he couldn't wait to get started on his clandestine quest of retribution.

SIX

RAILROAD RUSE

The weekly westbound train operating between Cheyenne and Evanston was on time. Smoke billowed from the chunky balloon stack. A bright red cowcatcher protruded in front to deter any beasts that might decide to wander onto the track. As with many engineers, Whistling Hank Wardle took great pride in his locomotive by decorating it in the manner of a Christmas tree.

Wardle's pride and joy was designated as a 4-4-0 with four swivelling front wheels and four driving wheels. He had named her the *Prairie Queen* in gold lettering. Wooden plugs gave the loco hooter its distinctive tone, which the engineer sounded frequently to announce his presence, usually at specified danger points. Whistling Hank was especially proud of his, which had achieved significant renown.

The loco's mournful hoot now echoed across the

SEND FOR THE BAD GUY!

flat terrain just before the train passed over the trestle bridge spanning the deep ravine of the Canadian River. Hundreds of these spidery wooden structures were needed to traverse the many cuttings encountered by the railroad companies. Tunnels likewise needed to be hacked through solid rock to make the country more accessible.

The hollow rumble informed the brakeman that they were now above the thrashing waters below. Unbeknown to the passengers up front, a faked robbery was afoot in the express car. Colonel Thruxton had arranged with the railroad company to stage the bogus heist in which the guard and conductor on the train were to play a vital role.

'Time to get ready, Mr Henry,' the brakeman announced. 'Another ten minutes and we'll have reached your drop-off point.'

'The name's Cracker Dan Spurlock,' the agent stressed firmly. 'Remember that when your report is filed. We have to make this look genuine. Any slip-ups and the whole thing will be sussed. And my life won't be worth a plugged nickel.'

'Sure thing ... Cracker.' The guy avidly nodded. 'Me and the conductor will play our parts. You can depend on us. Nobody else on board the train is in on the deception. Even the loco engineer knows nothing about what's going on. Knowing Whistling Hank, he'll cause a right fuss when he finds out.'

'You just play the innocent victim. Nothing is actually going to be stolen and nobody will get hurt,'

Spurlock stressed.

The change in tone of the rolling stock meant they had crossed the river and were now back on solid ground. 'I always heave a sigh of relief when I hear that sound,' the brakeman declared. 'Trundling over those flimsy wooden structures perched high above a ravine makes me nervous. It was only by sheer luck I wasn't on the train that derailed last year crossing the Arkansas River near Dodge City. That was one bad accident. Thirty people were killed and dozens injured. By chance I'd been transferred to a later train. It took a month before the service could be resumed. I'm sure glad I wasn't on that first train to cross …'

'Maybe we should leave this reminiscing for another time,' Cracker Dan reminded his collaborator. 'We must be nearly there now.'

The guy peered out of the window. The train was lumbering across a broad stretch of uninhabited wasteland. Sagebrush and mesquite dominated the arid terrain. It offered the ideal place to stage a train robbery and escape undetected. 'Best to wait until we're almost on that broken country up ahead where the grade rises to enter Muddy Gap,' the guy advised with thoughtful deliberation. 'The train will slow up, making it a sight easier for you to effect your escape without injury. Last thing you need is to be stuck out here with a broken leg.'

The fake robber nodded. 'And don't forget to give a detailed description of my appearance when the law questions you about the leader of the gang,' Cracker

Dan instructed the railroad brakeman. 'We have to make this look real. The law will be circulating a wanted dodger so it has to be detailed enough. And remember there were six of us in on it. We escaped with a strong box containing twenty thousand dollars after forcing you to open the safe.'

'Don't worry, I know what to say,' replied the eager railroad man, giving the tall BAD agent a close inspection. 'Six feet tall, one eighty pounds, straw-coloured hair and wearing a buckskin coat and black boots.'

'You could add that I was using a Whitney-Kennedy carbine too. Not many of them around. And a few random shots from you and your colleague once I've quit the train would help to create the right impression as well.' Spurlock hawked out a brittle guffaw. 'Aimed high, naturally.'

The brakeman joined in but there was little levity in his chortling. The time for the bogus robber's departure was now at hand and tensions were running high. This was the first time he had been involved in a train robbery, even if it was only a pretence. The guy shuddered to think what the real thing would be like.

Then another thought occurred to the bogus robber. 'I almost forgot to ask. I'll be on foot out there. Where's the nearest place to buy a horse?'

The brakeman pointed to a low line of broken hills. 'Over on the other side of Mount Steele, a guy called Saddleback Jim Widdows runs a horse ranch. You should reach it in a couple of hours easy.'

'Much obliged,' replied Spurlock. 'I ain't exactly

dressed for walking.'

'All right, this is it,' said the brakeman, dragging open the express car's sliding door.

Spurlock joined him. 'Wish me luck,' he said in a low voice. They shook hands.

'Glad to be of service,' the brakeman responded sincerely. 'I only hope you manage to pull this scam off. It can only be a matter of time before those Vender boys decide to up their game with the Central Pacific if'n they ain't caught soon.'

The wind tugged at Spurlock's hair as he leaned out of the open door and tossed out the iron-bound strong box. Moments later he followed. Hitting the hard ground on the run, he tucked his head in and rolled across the sand. Shouts from the disappearing train registered in his numbed brain. Shots rang out as the two railroad confederates made their valued contribution to the subterfuge.

Startled passengers leaned out of the windows, wondering at the source of the unexpected commotion. Scrambling behind some rocks, he drew his pistol and made his own badly aimed response.

It was the perfect spot to leave the train. An engineer would never stop the train on the up-grade as it would be too difficult to restart. Soon after it disappeared from view into Muddy Gap, Spurlock sucked in a deep breath. A swift look around revealed that, except for a curious prairie dog, he was alone. From here on Drew Henry would need to adopt the ruthless persona of a train robber if'n he was to successfully infiltrate the Vender Gang.

It was a tall order, but one that he relished. It felt good to be back in the guise of a BAD boy once again. He drew his pistol and blasted the strong box lock asunder. Inside was a token amount of just over three thousand dollars, most of which he stashed in his saddle-bag. It was all in hundred-dollar bills. A few were deliberately scattered about to give the impression of being missed in the dash to leave the scene of conflict.

He tossed a glance towards Mount Steele. From down here it looked much further away than on the train. A couple of hours now seemed way too optimistic. No use grumbling about it now. He set off in the direction indicated. Within minutes he realized that riding boots were definitely not designed with long foot marches in mind. As such it took the rest of the day before the newly created train robber limped across the threshold of the bronc-busting outfit run by Jim Widdows.

The bronc peelers operating the spread got the shock of their lives when the lone traveller stumbled into their midst. 'Where in blue blazes did you spring from?' Widdows exclaimed reaching for his revolver. 'More to the point, what you doing out here on foot?'

Spurlock slumped into a chair. His face creased in pain as he tugged off his boots. 'My horse broke a leg,' he winced, rubbing at the raw flesh of his lacerated feet. 'He slipped while crossing the railroad near the Canadian Bridge. I had to shoot him. This saddle-bag and my shooting irons were the only things I could carry.'

'Man, that must be all of twelve miles off,' chipped in the surprised cook, who was dishing out plates of stew. 'You were lucky to find us, mister.'

'That grub sure smells mighty tempting. I'm starving.' The newcomer was drooling at sight of the simple yet wholesome fair. He was plumb tuckered out.

But Saddleback Jim Widdows was still not convinced. 'I'd be obliged fella if'n you'd hand over your hardware.' The boss wrangler held out his hand. A gritty regard informed the newcomer that a refusal would mean no food and no welcome. 'We can't be too careful out here in the wilds. Only last month, I had three fresh broke mustangs stolen. The jaspers what took 'em must have sneaked in after dark.'

Spurlock complied. He was given no choice in the matter, although he readily understood the guy's wariness of strangers. Unbuckling the gun-belt, he handed it over along with the carbine.

'You can have 'em back when you leave,' Widdows replied, handing the guns over to Buster Chilcott, the oldest of the horse breakers. 'Lock these away in my office.'

'Sure thing, boss,' the bow-legged little guy said, shuffling off in that rolling gait characteristic of men who had spent their lives in the saddle.

'Give the guy a plate, Panhandle,' the boss instructed, now more relaxed. 'He looks all in.' He also pushed a jug of homemade beer across the table. 'Help yourself, stranger. You can bunk down here until you're ready to leave. Panhandle is a dab hand at treating injuries. He can sort your feet out when you've eaten. Seems to me you could do with a good night's sleep.'

'I ain't arguing there. These boots sure weren't made for walking that far.' And he meant it. 'If'n you're worried about me being on foot, I have enough dough to buy one of your horses,' Spurlock emphasized, heartily tucking in to the plateful of stew and dumplings. 'The name's Dan Spurlock. I'm heading west towards the Wind River country to do some hunting. They tell me there's plenty of deer in the hills up that way. The army pays good money for deer meat.'

Widdows then went on to introduce the others who were present. 'There's another guy on the payroll looking after some unbroken mustangs we've corralled in a narrow draw to the east of here.'

'This grub sure is going down a treat,' Spurlock burbled between mouthfuls. 'Reckon you boys have gotten yourselves a kitchen magician in old Panhandle.' The grizzled cook preened and strutted around pleased as punch that somebody had finally recognized his efforts.

'Ike Cassidy here can fix you up with a decent mount when you're ready.' Widdows nodded towards a rough-hewn jasper who was vigorously mopping up the gravy on his plate. 'You can have that vacant bunk on the end.'

The salve applied to Spurlock's blistered feet worked a treat. Next morning, he felt almost as good as new. As well as the kitchen, old Panhandle certainly knew his way around a medicine chest. 'Much obliged for this,' he thanked the old guy. 'And the grub too. I hate to think what would have happened if'n I'd missed your place.'

'All part of the service, Dan.' The old guy grinned, enjoying the unaccustomed praise. 'I'll be sorry to see you go. These guys take me for granted,' he complained. 'It makes a nice change to have someone around who appreciates what I do for 'em.'

'Don't you listen to him,' interrupted a lean-limbed buster called Buff Greeley. 'He wouldn't want to be anywhere else. Like all old dudes, he enjoys nothing more than a good old grouse.' Panhandle huffed some, but offered no denial.

Much as he appreciated the hospitality displayed by Saddleback Jim Widdows and his outfit, Spurlock wanted to be on his way. The train robbery would have been reported by now and wanted dodgers issued. He needed to put the next part of the plan into action. Around mid-morning, when the other guys were rounding up a batch of wild broncs in the nearby hill country, the visitor made his farewells.

'I'll put in a good word for you to the army commander at Fort Platte,' he promised the leader of the outfit, shaking Widdows' hand. 'They are always looking to buy good horse flesh.'

SEVEN

BAITING THE TRAP

It was three days later that Cracker Dan Spurlock arrived in Rock Springs. He paused on the edge of the town to imbibe the general feel. Absorbing the ambience and character was a ploy that he always adhered to when entering a strange place. Such innate instincts had rarely failed him.

Rock Springs was typical of a myriad other such bergs growing up in the western frontier territories. Wooden structures predominated, with those in the middle embracing ornately carved facings. Mounds of sawn timber were everywhere, ready to furnish the bare bones of numerous buildings still under construction.

Most were single storey. Only the courthouse and hotel boasted an extra floor, this latter sporting a fenced veranda. Street lighting and a boardwalk on either side running the whole length of the main street were further testimonies to this being a place with a future.

And judging by the proliferation of cattle pens on the outskirts, beef on the hoof indicated the main source of its prosperity. As if to confirm this assumption, a group of cowboys hustled out of a saloon and mounted up. Yipping and heehawing, they galloped out of town. None of them gave the newcomer a second glance. That was just how he liked it. Slide into a new town unnoticed.

But what really caught the stranger's attention were the handful of elegant houses set back in their own grounds. They contrasted markedly with the amalgam of rough-hewn shacks scrabbling for room on the steepening pine-clad slopes on the opposite side of the valley. There were clearly some folks in Rock Springs who were making their pile. Could this be something to do with the Venders?

He would only find out by allowing his newly acquired persona to be made known to the outlaw gang. And the place to start was up ahead on the left side of the main street. He nudged the chestnut forward. All the while hawkish eyes panned every nook and cranny, adding to his perception of the town and its inhabitants.

The general store was run by Elias McVay and Son. And according to the sign board outside it catered for every household necessity, and more besides – *What we ain't got we can get.*

'We'll soon see whether that's for real,' the newcomer muttered under his breath while tying up.

He entered the establishment and peered around

at the wide array of goods. An older man, clearly Elias McVay, was serving a young woman. He was grey haired with a thick moustache and in his middle years. His son was stocking the shelves at the back with some freshly delivered tinned goods.

Spurlock's eyes widened. He couldn't help but notice that the only other customer beside himself was no plain Jane. Undeniably pretty would have been his candid judgement. An appreciative gaze lingered over the engaging tableau. Blonde tresses swirling around her slim shoulders were held in place by a green velvet bow. She was wearing range gear, which indicated the girl was likely from one of the local ranches. The tight jeans and straining shirt accentuated the slim figure.

'Could you serve this gentleman, Angus?' the owner called across to his son. 'I'm busy at the moment.'

The boy turned around, only now seeing the newly arrived customer. An adept eye ran over the newcomer's trail-weary appearance. Straight away Angus McVay put him down as a drifter in search of work on one of the ranches.

'What can I get for you, sir?' the clerk asked, climbing down from the ladder.

With great reluctance, Spurlock dragged his eyes away from the vision of beauty. She was a sight better to look at than the spotty-faced kid hovering nearby.

'I need some .45–.60 cartridges that will fit this Whitney-Kennedy carbine,' Spurlock said, lifting the gun onto the counter. He would now be able to determine whether the store's claim held water. 'I'm hoping to do some hunting in the hills around here. I here tell there's plenty of deer up in the pine forests.'

'There certainly is,' replied the clerk, having to quickly reassess the tall stranger. A quizzical eye studied the long gun. 'We don't see many of these calibre firearms in Sweetwater County. Most fellas use the .44 Winchester or Sharps for hunting.'

'I had a Sharps, but I prefer the Whitney,' Spurlock replied, rubbing the rosewood stock. 'Guess it's what you get used to. And I figure the Whitney is more accurate for long range shooting. It has a lighter frame as well.'

Angus McVay shrugged, being no firearms expert. He then called across to his father. 'Do we have any .45 cartridges for the Whitney, Pa?'

'On the second shelf over to your left,' came back the immediate reply. 'But we ain't got many. No call for them around here.'

'I'll take what you have then,' replied an impressed Dan Spurlock, reaching into his billfold and extracting a wedge of notes. 'How much will that be?'

The boy totted up the total. 'That will be seven dollars and fifty cents, please.' He was somewhat startled to be presented with a hundred-dollar bill. 'Erm ... don't you have any less?' he stammered out. Spurlock concealed a smile. This was probably the first time the kid had seen anything above a twenty.

Spurlock shrugged as he riffled through the wedge of similar denomination notes. 'Sorry, that's the smallest I have.'

The boy went across and gave the note to his father. McVay studied it carefully while appraising the owner. He was not best pleased at having to give out a heap of small change. But the customer was always right. So he pasted a forced smile onto his grizzled features and handed over the pile of change.

'Guess that almost clears me out,' he guffawed trying unsuccessfully to laugh the irritation off. 'You'll have to go across to the bank and see if Mr Mawdsley will supply us with some more change, Angus.' The order was delivered in a restrained manner that left the culprit in no doubt as to the storekeeper's view of the matter.

Spurlock merely deposited the three boxes of cartridges in his saddle-bag as if nothing untoward had occurred.

The girl had finished her business and was about to pay. Turning his back on the object of his annoyance, McVay apologized to the patiently waiting customer with a genuine smile. 'Will that be all, Miss Vender?' the proprietor ingratiated himself while bagging up the purchases.

'For today thank you, Mr McVay,' she replied brightly, not having been aware of the disagreement with the other customer. Any sudden interest concerning the new arrival went unheeded. Gathering up her goods, the young woman made to leave.

Quick as a flash, Dan Spurlock was by her side. 'Mind if'n I help you out, miss?' he said, removing his hat while offering the girl his most dazzling smile. This was a stroke of luck that he had no intention of rejecting. Being a particularly fetching young woman played no part in his actions. Or so his conscience purported.

For the briefest of moments, the old Drew Henry felt a pang of guilt. His wife was not long in her grave. Should he be even contemplating a flirtatious liaison? He quickly convinced himself that getting to know a member of the Vender clan was all in the line of duty. And perhaps it would not be such an odious chore after all.

Without waiting for an answer from the girl, he picked up the heaviest box and headed for the door. Angus McVay scowled. He had been hoping to help the delectable Ruth Vender. But this guy had beaten him to the punch. All he could do now was hold the door open. A mere lackey's job.

Spurlock ignored the kid. His whole attention was focussed on the clearly grateful Ruth Vender. He could barely credit his luck. In Rock Springs for less than an hour and already he was in contact with the Vender clan.

'My wagon is over yonder,' the girl purred in a voice flowing like liquid chocolate while she led the way across the street. 'Could you bring the other things please, Angus?' she called back to the miffed clerk while flouncing off. Hips swaying provocatively, Ruth was completely unaware of the effect her innocent performance was having on the male onlookers.

Spurlock had to shake off the mixed messages that now swirled around inside his head. A notorious gang of robbers to infiltrate, and with a dame like this in their midst. It was a mind-blowing situation into which he had stumbled. Was she a member of the gang? He could barely credit that such an appealing prospect could transform herself into a ruthless desperado. Yet such a prospect had happened once before. Belle Sherman the Outlaw Queen was a case in point.

'Do you live nearby, miss?' he blithely asked. The innocuous comment was meant to winkle out her status in the notorious family.

'I live on a ranch about an hour's ride from here with my brothers,' she replied. 'Since our parents were taken by the fever, I've kept house for them. I only come into town once a week for supplies. There are more than usual this time. It was my good fortune that you were around to help me out.'

The alluring smile hinted at a little more than mere gratitude for this handsome stranger's help. Spurlock's eyes lit up. A lock of hair had slipped across her face. With great difficulty he resisted the temptation to push it aside. He forced his mind back to the matter under consideration.

So she was not married and didn't appear on the surface to be involved in the notorious depredations of her kinfolk. That said, she must be condoning their nefarious activities. Or was it just filial loyalty? He would certainly enjoy finding out in due course.

While loading up Ruth Vender's wagon, two hard cases emerged from the Big Horn saloon. Scooter Biggs and his buddy had been having a drink and were on their way back to the ranch.

'Who's the guy over yonder talking to Ruth?' Biggs rasped out.

'Never seen him before,' replied Robey. 'But that smirk on his kisser sure ain't one you would hand out to your ma.'

'And she seems to be lapping up the attention.'

'Cain ain't gonna be too pleased.' Biggs hitched up his gun-belt and stepped down into the rutted street. 'He don't like her talking to strangers. Reckon we ought to show him the quickest way out of town?'

'My thinking entirely, pard.'

The two outlaws strolled purposefully across the street. 'This guy bothering you, Miss Vender?' rapped Biggs, resting a glowering gaze on the tall stranger. He didn't wait for a reply. 'Take your goods and get back to the ranch. This fella is just leaving, ain't you, mister?'

Spurlock took a step back. 'Now that all depends on the lady,' he replied with casual ease. 'Am I hassling you, miss?'

Ruth Vender frowned at the two men. Her response was frosty and blunt. 'You guys have no business ordering me around. I'll talk to whomsoever I want. Now leave me alone and get back to the ranch otherwise I'll tell my brothers about your high-handed attitude.'

Robey was not phased. 'It's Cain who told us to look out for you. He don't like you associating with riff-raff.' The sneering rebuke was a direct challenge to the stranger to put up or shut up.

Spurlock's right eye lifted. So these critters were

also part of the Vender Gang. Well, here was a good opportunity to make his presence known. Not quite how he had planned it. But he'd been pushed into a corner. These jaspers wanted a tussle. And he was the guy to oblige them. Not wasting any more time on a pointless swap of insults, he took decisive action. A blunt-edged straight left shot out catching the first tough on the button. Axell Robey fell back clutching at his blooded snout. A right hook finished the critter off.

His buddy stepped aside and made to draw his pistol.

But Spurlock was ready for him. His own revolver stopped the antagonist in his tracks. An ugly grin, lacking any warmth, bore into the startled outlaw. 'Now unhook them gun-belts pronto. Either that or fill your hands. Although I wouldn't rate your chances of walking out of here alive if'n you make the wrong choice.'

Robey snarled as he lay sprawled in the dirt. But he was out of the running. Spurlock's double-fisted hammer blows had knocked the stuffing out of him. Bigg's on the other hand was far more circumspect. He could recognize an experienced gunfighter when he saw one. And that hogleg was pointing right at his chest.

'OK, mister, you've gotten the drop on us this time.' Nonetheless, he was no tenderfoot himself. A final parting shot made it clear the ruckus would not be overlooked. 'But you ain't heard the last of this. Not by a long shot.'

'Just get your buddy over to the sawbones,' was Spurlock's curtly delivered advice. 'He's giving the town a bad name spreading all that red stuff over the boardwalk.'

Snarling and grumbling like a pair of cowed mutts, the two men stumbled off up the street. Spurlock watched until they were out of sight before resuming his conversation with the delectable Ruth Vender as if nothing untoward had occurred.

'Perhaps I might see you again sometime, miss?' he said, slotting the last box onto the wagon. 'I'll be around for a couple of days before heading off to the hunting grounds. Or perhaps I could drop by and visit you at your ranch.'

A wary frown darkened the smooth complexion. 'I d-don't think that would be a very g-good idea, Mr ...?' she stammered out. Ruth was bewildered by the recent outburst of violence right in front of her. 'And I don't even know your name.'

'That's easily rectified,' drawled the mysterious stranger. 'Dan Spurlock at your service, ma'am.' He removed his hat with a chivalric flourish and bowed.

Ruth climbed onto the wagon. She needed time to think. 'I'm sure we will meet up again soon,' she said, urging the team into motion without looking back.

'I'll look forward to it,' came back the confident reply as she rode off.

EIGHT

CRACKED!

The three conniving officials from Rock Springs were in a sour frame of mind when they arrived at the Vender ranch. They had ridden hard once news about the train robbery had been reported. Such a heist in their bailiwick could only have been instigated by the Vender Gang. But where had the cheating rats secured the essential information concerning the valuable shipment without their vital contribution?

Features hardened measurably as they knocked on the door. It was Cain Vender himself who opened the door.

'What do you guys want?' His scowling face offered no welcome to his three cronies. They were clearly not expected. The next job was only in the planning stage and no meeting had yet been arranged. The gang leader's mind was taken up with the stranger reported by his two henchman the previous day. According to them, Ruth had been rather too smitten with the jasper. Harsh words had passed between them. The last thing he needed at the moment was these three varmints giving him grief.

'We reckon you've been holding out on us, Cain,' snapped Judge Gideon Fitzroy, pushing his way into the room. 'We're all in this together. Any jobs you decide to pull have to be agreed by us first. Seems to us like you've been breaking the rules.' The portly gavel-tapper prodded a finger at the accused outlaw.

'So we want our cut,' butted in the prosecuting attorney, stepping forward. 'Twenty thousand bucks is no mean sum.' He also gave his prodding digit some forceful action. 'We never figured you guys were up to robbing trains. Looks like we were wrong. So what have you to got to say for yourself?'

'And it better be good,' added the judge for good measure.

Cain was completely bewildered by this blatant accusation. He even ignored the prodding. For the moment he was lost for words.

Sheriff Speakman used Cain's hesitation to push his way to the fore. 'We want our cut of all the jobs you pull, Cain,' he averred. 'That was the deal when we went into business together.'

'I don't know what the heck you guys are talking about,' Cain protested vehemently. 'We haven't pulled no train job. Where in tarnation did you get this crack-pot idea?'

Hearing the raised voices in the other room, Abel

and Hog made their presence felt. 'What's all the darned ruckus in here?'

'These crazy galoots are accusing us of robbing a train and keeping them in the dark. Did you boys ever hear of such a hare-brained scheme?' He coughed out a strangled guffaw that lacked any sense of amusement.

'That sure ain't down to us,' Abel attested. 'But now you come to mention it, a train job don't seem such a bad idea.'

The three men were not convinced. 'If you didn't pull it, then who did?' Judge Fitzroy pushed a wanted poster into the hands of Abel Vender. 'This description of their leader fits you perfectly.'

Cain grabbed a hold of the dodger. 'And it could fit any one of a hundred guys around here.' The creases around his eyes hardened along with his tone. 'I'm telling you straight, we had nothing to do with this.' The other two brothers backed him up with equally hard-boiled resilience.

The three officials were wavering. It was a conundrum that needed solving, and quickly, as Elmer Hyde firmly declared. 'This needs sorting out. We can't have some rogue gang operating in Sweetwater County. It's bad for business.'

'Not to mention your pockets,' interjected the cynical voice of Ruth Vender who had been listening in behind the door. 'Maybe now you critters will decide to call it a day and do the job you're paid for instead of fleecing the good citizens of this county. You ought to be ashamed of yourselves.'

'You aren't going to squeal on us are you, Ruth?' enquired the alarmed prosecuting attorney. 'The dough that your brothers are making will pay for a life of luxury in no time. Just a couple more jobs and we'll all be able to retire to a life on easy street.'

The woman hawked out a sarcastic gripe. 'No need to worry. I'll keep my mouth shut … for now. But any more killing and we'll have to see whether blood is thicker than water.'

'That guy in Lander was an unlucky shot. But with Joey getting hit as well, I figure we're even,' Abel averred, giving his sister a sour look. 'Anyway it's getting close to chow time. And Hog here is getting edgy.' That quip at the expense of the corpulent Esau Vender appeared to lessen the build-up of tension.

It was Judge Fitzroy who brought the conversation back to the serious issue on all their minds. 'There still remains the unsolved mystery as to who did rob that train. If you fellas are as innocent as you claim, it's in all our interests to flush them out.'

Any further discussion was postponed as the steady drub of hooves indicated that somebody was approaching the ranch. Elmer Hyde was nearest to the window. 'It's a lone rider. I ain't never seen the guy before. Must be a stranger.'

The others joined him. Suspicion was written all over their faces. All that is except for Ruth, whose eyes lit up. She was the only one to recognize the newcomer. 'It's Mr Spurlock. He helped me with my shopping yesterday,' she said breezily and without further ado went outside to greet the Good Samaritan.

Cain tried to pull her back. But she was too quick for him. He growled out a curse under his breath. As far as he was concerned, any stranger to the Vender ranch spelt trouble. He watched from the window as his sister stepped down off the porch to greet the newcomer. To the mistrustful outlaw, she was being uncommonly sociable. He could not hear the tête-à-tête, but the guy was being far too attentive for his liking.

'I didn't expect to see you again so soon,' Ruth said as the rider stepped down from his horse.

'I've rented an old cabin up in the hills over yonder.' A languid hand indicated the splay of pine forest to the west. 'Your place is on the way so I figured to call by and return these.' He lifted the pair of gun-belts hanging from the saddle horn. 'Those two guys should have cooled off by now. But if'n I'm truthful, it was just an excuse to see you again.'

Ruth failed to contain the flush of rouge enveloping her cheeks. Out of nowhere this handsome stranger had come into her life. She was lost for words, tongue-tied and feeling a mite shy.

Dan Spurlock's warm smile sent a shiver down her spine. 'I stayed at the hotel in Rock Springs last night after I'd been out to see the cabin with the real estate guy.'

'That must be the old Stanton place,' Ruth declared. 'Chuck Stanton was a hunter like you before he was attacked and killed by a grizzly while out stalking.' Her concern for the safety of this man was evident as she hurried on. 'They found the remains of his body down a ravine. You will be careful, won't you?' she added, clutching his arm.

'Don't you worry about me, ma'am,' he stressed. 'Ain't no darned bear going to catch Dan Spurlock on the hop.' He took off his hat before making his next proposal, one which found the confident newcomer himself somewhat awkward. 'I don't know if'n you've heard but there's a barn dance being held out at the Flying V ranch next Saturday. I'd be mighty honoured if'n you'd accompany me.'

Ruth's heart skipped a beat. She knew all about the dance. Angus McVay had asked her to go but she had made excuses. To be the guest of Dan Spurlock would be the answer to all her dreams.

But she never got the chance to elicit a positive response. Cain Vender had seen enough. And he didn't like what he saw. Not one bit. 'She ain't going nowhere with you, mister.' The blunt announcement was delivered with one hand resting on the butt of his revolver. 'Now mount up and clear off, pronto.'

The languid smile slipped from Spurlock's craggy features. 'And who might you be to order me around?'

'I'm her brother and this is my spread.' Abel and Hog had now joined their brother on the porch. 'Strangers ain't welcome here.' The three men scowled at Spurlock, who displayed no intimidation from their threatening manner.

'That ain't a very a friendly greeting for a new neighbour.'

'I'm no friend of your'n, mister. And I don't have to be neighbourly,' growled the gang leader. 'So mount up and ride out of here.'

'Now that all depends on the lady,' Spurlock replied, nonchalantly replacing his hat and making a point of keeping his right hand away from the holstered revolver. 'After all, it's her I came to see, not you.' Not entirely a truthful statement; he also wanted a closer look at the rats who killed his brother.

Ruth's back straightened. Her pert nose twitched disdainfully at her hovering kinfolk. 'And I'd be more than happy to accompany you to the dance, Mr Spurlock. Nobody is going tell me who I can or can't see.'

Cain's mouth twisted in a resentful grimace. His whole body was ready to throw out a challenge. Spurlock recognized the signs of an impending show-down. That was the last thing he needed. 'Don't worry I'm going,' he declared, mounting up. 'Perhaps we'll meet up in town soon to discuss the arrangement … this time in private, Miss Vender.'

'I'll look forward to it,' was the girl's perky reply.

All her brothers could do was stand there, fuming impotently. Back inside the house, Judge Fitzroy was the first to break the taut silence. 'That guy could be trouble. We need to keep an eye on him. He's too darned cocky for my liking.'

The discussion surrounding the mysterious train robbery was resumed. Various theories were suggested and discarded. An hour later they were no further forward. But at least, the three officials had been persuaded that the Venders were not involved. They left the ranch hoping that it was just a one-off occurrence, a band of outlaws passing through the territory.

A couple of days passed with no further incidents. The three men were sitting in the judge's quarters above the courthouse in Rock Springs.

It was Elmer Hyde who posed the view that the failure of the Lander job and this recent incursion by unknown lawbreakers meant their illicit situation was becoming precarious. 'Questions have been asked in the town council about why the Vender Gang is being allowed to operate with impunity in Sweetwater County. I made excuses that there was too much territory for one man to cover.'

'Did they buy it?' asked the judge.

'Only after it was agreed that a new deputy be appointed,' the prosecutor replied.

'So that's how I got lumbered with an oaf like Plug Yancy,' grumbled the sheriff.

'He may be lacking in the brain department,' countered Hyde firmly, 'but at least he's one of our own boys. McVay was trying to have his son imposed on us.'

That said, they were all well aware that time was not on their side. Judge Fitzroy voiced the concern that was in all their minds. 'We're up for re-election in a couple of months. And the likelihood is that we'll all be voted out of office.'

A mood of despondency settled over the three miscreants. The sheriff's fingers drummed monotonously on the desk top. His thick eyebrows met in the middle of a furrowed brow, giving the impression of a weasel having taken up residence.

'Do you have to make that racket?' complained Fitzroy, scratching at a wart on his nose. 'It's giving me a goldarned headache.'

'It helps me to think,' shot back the starpacker, leering at the judge's ugly bulge.

'Well go think outside,' was the curt response as Fitzroy continued picking at his snout. 'Or better still why not apprehend some litter dropper for a change?'

'Give it a rest you two,' the sartorial Hyde admonished his colleagues, brushing an imaginary speck of dust off his sharply creased trousers. 'Start arguing among ourselves and we're done for. What we need is one good job. Then we can all retire with our billfolds full of dough. Pull it off and it won't matter if'n we lose our jobs.'

'That Saving and Loan Company we sussed out in Granger will make us all rich,' Fitzroy remarked, wiping his nose with a handkerchief. 'But I don't trust Cain Vender one little bit. I still ain't properly won over that his gang had nothing to do with that damned train job.'

'Then maybe we should have Yancy ride along to make sure we get our cut,' the prosecutor suggested. 'He can keep an eye on the share-out.'

'That guy ain't had no dealings with bank robberies,' the judge objected. 'He's OK hustling store tenants late with rents. But letting him in on something like this could be more trouble than it's worth.'

At that moment there was a knock on the office door and Plug Yancy came in. The ugly tough strutted over, his shiny new badge of office clearly on display. 'This note has just been sent over from the bank,' he said, handing the message to Fitzroy. 'The manager said it was urgent.'

Fitzroy's eyes widened as he read it through.

'Any reply?' enquired the messenger.

The judge merely shook his head, a prodding thumb signalling the lackey to depart.

'Some'n wrong?' asked Speakman, picking up on his associate's grim look once the door had closed. The judge handed the note across. The sheriff read it aloud. 'A hundred-dollar bill confirmed as one of those found at the scene of the Laramie-Evanston train robbery handed in by Elias McVay.'

'Looks like the robbers mistakenly left some dough beside the track in their hurry to escape,' deduced the excited sheriff. 'I got a feeling that's gonna be their downfall.'

All of a sudden, the downcast mood lifted. Once again the future looked bright. This revelation was the break they had been after. Find out who passed it over and there was a good chance that person was one of the robbers.

'If'n we can catch these jaspers, it'll be a feather in our caps,' Speakman enthused.

Scrambling to their feet, the three men hurried off down the street to interview the unwitting storekeeper.

Being the prosecutor, Elmer Hyde took it upon himself to do the probing. 'We were wondering how you came into possession of this hundred-dollar bill, Elias.'

The old guy considered the query for a moment. But there was little to think about. Hundred-dollar bills were only handled for large consignments of goods, rarely if ever on a day-to-day basis. 'A stranger came by wanting some cartridges for his rifle. He didn't have any smaller bills. In fact, he pulled out a whole wad of them and just peeled one off cool as you please. You don't forget that in a hurry.'

'What did he look like?' pressed the sheriff.

'Tall guy with fair hair wearing a buckskin coat,' replied McVay without any hesitation. 'He helped Ruth Vender with her goods. They seemed to be getting mighty friendly. The cartridges were for a Whitney-Kennedy carbine. Luckily we had some in stock. My boast is what McVay and Son ain't got …'

'Yeh, we know all about that,' piped in the judge irritably.

'Anything wrong?' the storekeeper asked.

'No, nothing at all.' Hyde hastened to reassure the guy. Last thing they needed was for him to become suspicious. 'The bank brought it to our attention. Just a general enquiry is all. Anyway, much obliged for your help.'

Once outside, Sheriff Speakman iterated what they were all thinking. 'It has to be that guy who called at the Vender spread.'

'He's taken the old Stanton place up on Pathfinder Bluffs,' added the prosecutor.

'Then we'd better get up there pronto and ask this Spurlock character what he knows about the hundred-dollar bill that has so conveniently come into his possession,' Judge Fitzroy declared.

'And he better have the right answers,' growled Speakman.

NINE

INFILTRATION

Dan Spurlock had been kicking his heels since leaving the Vender spread. He was becoming impatient for something to happen. That hundred-dollar bill was the bait that should lure the rats out of their holes. The railroad authorities should have circulated the numbers of the stolen bills to all the banks in the territory by now. It was only a matter of time before they paid him a visit.

This waiting around was getting on his nerves. Sure he had the barn dance to look forward to on Saturday night with Ruth Vender. But his priority had to be nailing these varmints once and for all so that Cole could rest easy in his grave.

The previous day he had gone to the local cemetery where his brother had received a pauper's burial. Great care had to be exercised to ensure he was not observed. A lump formed in his throat on seeing the wooden marker stuck away in a weed-choked corner of the graveyard.

Only a few words were possible. The elder Henry's brow furrowed as he swore vehemently to bring the killers to justice and in so doing ensure Cole was given a fitting headstone to mark his passing. He stayed no more than a few minutes. The visit had proved to be too painful an experience. He left without a backward glance, continuing up into the hill country. The clandestine guise was consolidated by stalking a deer.

The pelt was now drying on a frame outside the cabin. Any callers would thus have no reason to doubt his legitimacy.

Spurlock was cleaning the Whitney inside when the thud of hoof beats assaulted his ears. His whole body stiffened. 'Looks like the varmints have fallen into the trap,' he muttered under his breath.

How he was going to play this had been tossed over in his mind a dozen times during the last few days. From a firm denial that he knew anything about the robbery to an indifferent acceptance – whatever he decided had to look good. Being too eager could raise their doubts that he was a notorious train robber new to Wyoming. Too much defiance could find him occupying a jail cell.

'You in there, Spurlock? I have a few questions that need answering.' The decision had been made that, as the official representative of law and order, Sheriff Speakman should take the lead. He tried making his request casual so as not to alarm the alleged robber.

He already knew that the new resident was at home. His horse was tied up outside. 'This is Sheriff Tash Speakman. As the local lawman, I always like to check out newcomers to the district. Mind if'n I come in?'

The door opened. Spurlock was met by five guns pointing his way. They were held by a set of grim-faced dudes he had never seen before. Two were well dressed in suits and neckties. The others wore standard range garb.

'We know all about you, Cracker Dan. Inside and keep your hand away from that rifle,' rapped Speakman, dismounting. 'You boys stay out here and keep your guns handy.' The sheriff indicated for the cabin's occupant to step back inside. He was accompanied by the judge and prosecutor.

Cracker Dan. So they knew his assumed nickname. It had not been mentioned at all during his brief sojourn in the district. Dan's heart lurched, his whole being tensed. Had these critters been in touch with the New Mexico authorities and learned that the real Spurlock was dead?

But the lawman's continued grilling convinced him that Colonel Thruxton had done his job well. Any query received regarding the deceased train robber must have been redirected to the office of the BAD organization in Laramie.

'This is Judge Fitzroy and prosecuting attorney, Elmer Hyde,' Speakman rapped out, his tone much sharper now they had the upper hand. 'We have good reason to believe you were involved in the robbery from the Evanston-Laramie train of twenty thousand dollars last week. So what have you to say for yourself?'

Spurlock heaved a gentle sigh of relief while affecting a look of shocked surprise. His mouth hung open. 'I don't know anything about a robbery. I'm a hunter hoping to provide fresh meat to the army. It's stored out back if'n you want proof that I'm on the level. You saw the drying pelt outside.'

'A cover story is all,' scoffed Hyde. 'You can't fool us with that.'

'If'n you're so innocent, how come you paid for some cartridges at McVay's store in Rock Springs with a hundred-dollar bill?' rapped Judge Fitzroy, waving the incriminating banknote in the accused man's face. 'We know that it's one of those from the train. So don't try and wheedle your way out. It was you that robbed the train, wasn't it?'

Spurlock lifted his hands. 'You got this all wrong, fellas. I earned that money fair and square.'

'Don't give me that,' the prosecutor butted in, shaking his meaty fist in the bogus outlaw's face. 'You made the mistake of leaving some of the notes at the scene of the crime and the numbers match with this one.' Hyde's pompous smirk challenged Spurlock to deny the charge. The bogus train robber had to curb his natural instinct to jump out of his seat and punch this turnip on the jaw. But that would be a bad move on his part. So he was forced to absorb the berating tirade. 'And no doubt we'll find some more when we search this place.'

Encouraged by their dominance of the situation, Judge Fitzroy joined in. 'You might as well own up now otherwise it will be the worse for you. Yancy and Duke are mighty handy with their fists when it comes to extracting information from reluctant prisoners.'

'You're facing a long prison sentence for this Spurlock,' the sheriff iterated, taking up the verbal cudgel. 'So where's the rest of your gang? One man couldn't have pulled that heist off alone.'

Spurlock's head drooped as if in surrender to the inevitable. The time had come to show his hand if he didn't want a beating. He had sussed out that Fitzroy was the guy who had most authority with this bunch of crooks. So it was the judge who needed persuading to adopt his plan of action.

'I ain't saying nothing in front of all you jaspers,' he declared firmly. 'You're the top man around here where the law's concerned. That right, Judge?' His firm gaze was fixed on the hovering legal eagle.

Fitzroy nodded.

'Then get rid of these turkeys and maybe we can talk.'

'You ain't in no position to start giving orders to us ...'

Hyde's vehement remonstration was cut short by a raised hand from Gideon Fitzroy, who puffed out his chest. It was a back-handed compliment from the outlaw to be recognized as the dominant personality in this shady conclave. 'You heard the man,' he snapped out. 'He wants to speak to the chief not the Indians.

Now wait outside until I call you back you in.'

Fitzroy's two associates bristled indignantly, but a caustic frown saw them backing out. Once the door was closed and the pair were alone, the judge rasped, 'OK, Spurlock, what do you have to say?'

'You've gotten me over a barrel here, Judge,' the prisoner confessed, generating his best hangdog expression. 'Soon as you discovered my identity, it was clear I couldn't hoodwink a smart guy like you.' The artificial praise was lapped up by the gullible adjudicator. 'And you're right. I did rob that train.'

'So where's the dough hidden?' the greedy critter interrupted. 'The report said that twenty thousand bucks were taken.'

'There's only three grand left,' Spurlock declared with an apologetic shrug of the shoulders. 'The dough was split six ways plus a cut for the railroad informant. The other guys hightailed it after we did the share-out. But I wanted to stick around and see what was on offer around here.'

Fitzroy gave the remark a sly grin. 'I know what's keeping you in Sweetwater, fella. And it's not the hope of easy pickings, unless you count the Vender gal. Your mistake was underestimating me and my associates. That was a durned foolish oversight to mislay those bills.'

Spurlock's face turned a brighter shade of red. 'Guess you're smarter than I figured, Judge. Ain't no fooling you.'

'And don't you forget it. Now how's about you

delivering up that cut of your'n? My associates and I need to recover some of that loot to prove we're not shirking our duty.' He hooked his thumbs into the lapels of his jacket, affecting a superior mien. 'And seeing as you're prepared to surrender peaceful like, I'll recommend a lenient sentence at your trial.'

Spurlock considered this magnanimous gesture for a moment. 'There is another option you could go for,' he finally suggested.

'And what's that?'

'It's about the informant I have inside the railroad company. And a superintendent no less. He knows about every load passing through Laramie by rail, from cattle and coal shipments ...' A brief pause followed to build up the expectation as his voice dropped to little more than a whisper. '... to hefty payrolls in hard currency.'

The BAD boy casually sat back in his seat and rolled a stogie. He lit up and blew out a perfect smoke ring, carefully inspecting the judge's reaction. He was not disappointed. Fitzroy was all ears now. His beady eyes exhibited an avaricious gleam. 'Go on then,' he pumped out, drawing closer.

'Now you could send me to jail,' the speaker continued in a lackadaisical manner. 'But that wouldn't be very profitable, would it? So what if'n I was to tell you that this guy has it on good authority that a hundred grand is being transported on the westbound Continental Flyer over to the army headquarters at Fort Bozeman?'

That was the sprat to catch a full-grown pike. And Judge Fitzroy snapped at the lure. 'And who is this alleged fairy godfather?'

A low chuckle rumbled in Spurlock's throat. 'No alleged about it. He's for real all right. But I'm kinda smart myself, Judge. Give you that vital information along with the carriage date and you won't need me anymore, will you?' He tossed a sly wink at the slavering toad. 'And to prove my good faith, I will agree to hand over my share of the Evanston haul. If'n it doesn't work out, at least you'll be a winner by three grand.'

He puffed on the stogie, allowing the portly official to mull over what had been placed on the table. 'So what do you say? Are you in or out?'

Fitzroy responded with a bit of chin stroking, humming and hawing to himself before delivering a perceptive nod of the head. 'OK you two, in here now,' he called out. The blunt order found the pair of second lieutenants hustling back inside the cabin. The two henchmen were left outside to mind the horses. As mere lackeys, what was about to be divulged was not for their hearing.

Fitzroy quickly apprised them both of the deal. Elmer Hyde's first reaction was wariness. 'You reckon we can trust this jasper?'

'For a share in a hundred grand, I'd throw in with the Devil himself,' blurted out Sheriff Speakman. 'I'm sure the judge's astute verdict in this matter is reliable.'

'So we're agreed, gentlemen?' Fitzroy asked his associates. 'We let Spurlock here organize this caper.'

'Sure thing, Judge,' was the reply from both men.

'So how about you handing over that three grand now, partner?' the judge smirked, holding out a pudgy hand.

Three pairs of hostile peepers skewered the pretender as he turned on his heel and strode across to the fireplace. There he removed a loose stone and reached into the exposed hole, removing a bag which he handed to Judge Fitzroy. 'It's all there,' he stressed when the guy slowly counted out the notes.

'It never does any harm to double check.' His thoughts had resurrected a suspicion that Cain Vender had been creaming off more than his due in recent jobs. Satisfied, he peeled off the requisite cut for each of his buddies. 'Just to make sure you're not trying to trick us, I want you to join the Venders on their next job. You're going to need them to pull off this train robbery of your'n. And it'll give you chance to get acquainted.'

'I don't think Cain Vender likes me very much,' Spurlock announced. 'He didn't take kindly to me asking his sister to the barn dance.'

'You leave the Venders to me,' Fitzroy pledged brusquely. 'Cain'll do exactly as I tell him. And if'n he kicks up a fuss, I'll make it a court order.'

That jocular piece of wisdom caused a deal of hilarity amongst his colleagues, with which Spurlock saw fit to join in.

'So when is this job happening, and what's the hit?' Spurlock had an ulterior motive for his enquiry. If'n he could get word to Colonel Thruxton in time, this bunch

SEND FOR THE BAD GUY!

of crooks could be hog-tied and branded without the need to organize a full-blown train robbery.

Fitzroy hawked out a garbled guffaw, stabbing a lumpy finger into his chest. 'Just like you, mister, I ain't falling for that one. You get the details as and when the time is right.'

'Just our way of ensuring that nothing goes wrong,' added Elmer Hyde.

Soon after, the deputation departed. Spurlock cracked a satisfied smile. He was well pleased with the way things had gone.

Saturday morning arrived with no further word about the imminent robbery. The monthly barn dance was due to be held at the Flying V that night. Spurlock was looking forward to escorting Ruth Vender. He fancied himself as a dancer. Gabby had never complained. And he reckoned his footwork would match that of anyone there. But he needed some new duds if'n he was to impress the girl.

As a result he was one of the first customers to enter the McVay emporium. A smart shirt and necktie would suffice. He could brush down his spare pants. Once he had, and given his boots a good polishing and shaven the thick wedge of fuzz off'n his face, no gal would be able to resist the strutting dandy. Although in truth the only person he was bothered about was Ruth.

They had already enjoyed a picnic together down by the creek. Much to the annoyance of Cain Vender. But short of imprisoning his feisty sister, there was little

96

he could do to scotch the burgeoning liaison. So far everything had been above board, no physical contact of an intimate nature. Although Dan had every intention of pushing their relationship on to the next stage at tonight's dance.

He was excited, like the cat that got the cream. And it felt good. He didn't feel any guilt at showing interest in another woman. His beloved Gabby would never be forgotten and he would always love her. But it was now time to move on. A major quandary was his dedication to destroying the Vender Gang and avenging his brother's murder at their hands.

As a member of the same family, Ruth was a different proposition. He did not want to hurt her. Although as the saying goes, you can't fry eggs without breaking them. How would she react after learning of his true intentions? It was a dilemma that would have to be faced sometime.

But not tonight. Saturday was for dancing and having a good time.

He paid for the clothes and left the store, whistling a tune as he walked up the street, such were his high spirits. A voice from behind called out his name. He turned to see a guy he did not recognize hurrying towards him. He was lean of limb and wearing stained overalls. The smell of chickens was overpowering. This had to be Sam Vender, the only male member of the clan to merit a fair hearing.

'I'm glad to have caught you, Mr Spurlock,' the guy said, tugging at the hat in his hand. His manner was rather hesitant, as if wary of making this approach. 'I know you're kinda sweet on our Ruth, and I also know she feels the same. In fact, if my guess is right, she's falling in love with you. Ruth's a stubborn girl, strong willed. And much as she detests the type of life her brothers have followed, family loyalty means a lot to her.' He stopped, not sure how to present the crux of his appeal.

'If'n you are wanting to know whether my intentions towards your sister are honourable, the answer is a resounding yes,' Spurlock butted in with vigour.

'It's not that. I know you wouldn't deliberately hurt her. But if'n she stays with Cain and the others, who knows what will happen. What I'm asking is that you take her away from here, some place that she'll be safe. As things stand at the moment, she might soon become tarred with the same brush.'

Spurlock was taken aback by this supplication. It was something that had not occurred to him. He had a job to do. Perhaps when it was completed he could indeed accede to Sam Vender's wishes. There again, with the Venders out of the picture, there would be no need to leave.

'I have some business to conclude supplying meat to the army,' he said. 'When that is finished, I will certainly give your suggestion some serious thought. But it'll have to be her decision.'

'That's all I wanted to hear, Mr Spurlock.' Sam heaved out a sigh of gratitude. 'It's Ruth's safety that I am concerned with here. I can look after myself if'n things take an ugly turn. I appreciate your understanding.'

He set his hat straight and moved off about his business. The reek of chickens left in his wake brought a smile to Spurlock's face. He called out to the farmer. 'Are you intending to go to the dance tonight, Sam?'

Vender stopped and turned around. 'I ain't been before,' he conceded, 'but I might well give it a try.'

'In that case, I'd recommended a visit to the barber's across the street.' The advice was accompanied by a light-hearted grin to show he meant no offence. 'You might also wish to try out his bath tub out back or the gals will be giving you a wide berth.'

And with that he made to depart. The new duds were stuck in his saddle-bag. Mounting up, he headed down the street back to the cabin. But one unresolved question kept rearing its ugly head. How was Ruth going to react when she learned that he had thrown in with her brothers? He could not risk telling her the truth until the whole business was over. And that could mean a rope's end for her kinfolk.

Once again he pushed the problem to the back of his mind.

It was early afternoon when Dan Spurlock rode out of Rock Springs back to his cabin. His mind was now fully focussed on the dance that coming night. So he failed to heed the five riders approaching. Only when a gruff voice called out for him to haul rein were his thoughts jerked back to the present.

Cain Vender and his boys had spread themselves across the trail.

TEN

ACROSS THE DIVIDE

'Hold up there, Spurlock. I want words with you.'

It was Cain Vender who had spoken. And judging by his tone, what he had to say was no pleasant greeting between friends. But Fitzroy had been insistent. Much as Cain had tried arguing against the official's ruling, the order stood. And it was the judge who had the power to dictate terms, a fact that irked the gang leader but which he was impotent to change. As long as the lucrative jobs kept being supplied, he would have to play ball.

Cain was adamant, however, that a time would come when it was he who would be giving the orders. But for now his hands were tied.

'I don't like you, Spurlock,' the gang boss grunted. 'Not one little bit. But I'm a businessman, and the job comes before personal feelings. The fact is I've been told you're a useful guy to have along for what I have in mind.' Spurlock remained tight-lipped, concealing a smile. Judge Fitzroy had clearly issued his 'court order'. 'And you ain't too slow with your fists neither.'

Biggs and Robey gritted their teeth, straining at the leash. It was clear from the arrows of hate being loosed his way that they would like nothing more than to gun him down right there in the open.

Abel Vender held a similar opinion of this menacing interloper. 'First time we met at the ranch, I knew there was something shifty about you,' growled Abel. 'And I was right. That story about being a hunter was all hogwash, wasn't it?'

'I'll do the talking,' snapped Cain, cutting his brother short. The judge had given explicit orders that Spurlock was to be included in the forthcoming heist. 'We can always use a solid gun hand who don't panic easy. There's a job been planned to take the Savings and Loan Company over in Granger. It's on the far side of Flaming Gorge. You up for that?'

Spurlock deliberately gave the suggestion some thought before replying. He didn't want to appear too eager. 'Maybe, if'n it pays well.'

'You'll receive a fair cut, same as the rest of the boys,' the gang leader shot back.

Still the BAD boy prevaricated. 'So when does it go ahead?'

'We're heading that way now.'

Spurlock was stunned. The surprise registered on his face as he spluttered out, 'That's mighty short notice. I need time to organize things. Get my gear together.'

More important, by going along with these guys, he would miss the dance that night. What would Ruth think when he never turned up? That was the first thing that jumped into his head. It was a quandary that could only ever have one answer.

But Drew Henry was here to do a job and avenge his brother Cole. That had to come before anything else. Only then did he realize that no warning could be sent to Thruxton to organize an ambush. He would have to go along and play it by ear. None of these qualms registered on the craggy façade, which remained rigid and inscrutable.

'It's a two-day ride over the Divide through Fontenelle Gap. We need to be in Granger first thing on Monday morning,' Cain stressed, pushing his horse forward. His warped features registered irritation. 'That's when there will be most dough in the bank vault. You're packing a bedroll and hardware. That's all you need. You can share our grub. Now are you in or out?'

With five guns ready and eager to fill his hide with lead should he refuse, there was only one response. Not that he had any intentions of backing out. This was his big chance to join the Venders and make his presence felt. It was a pity about missing the dance. A suitable excuse would need to be fabricated to explain his absence.

'No need to get edgy,' Spurlock reacted frostily. 'Of course I'm in. Dan Spurlock never shucks the chance to make some easy dough.'

'Glad to hear it. OK boys, let's ride,' Cain snapped

out, swinging his mount west along the trail heading for the Big Sandy foothills and the Great Divide.

The gang arrived in Granger in pairs. Abel and Scooter Biggs were the front markers. Their job was to make sure there were no unexpected problems in evidence such as an army patrol passing through, or the posting of guards around the bank. With allegedly forty grand sitting in the vault, the manager might well have taken extra safety precautions.

'Don't look like they've got any extra men around,' Abel observed while casually leaning on the hitching rail.

'Should I take a walk round the other side just to make sure?' Biggs asked.

'Good idea,' replied his sidekick. 'The rest of the boys ought to be here in another half hour. Then we can get to work. It's this waiting around that I don't like.'

Biggs nodded and moved off in a laid-back saunter. He had been gone five minutes when Hog and Robey arrived. A curt nod of recognition was all that passed between them. The newcomers tied off their mounts on the opposite side of the street up town of the bank. They pretended to be checking their saddle fastenings. A moment later, Biggs returned to confirm there were no guards around the back, which was where the raid would take place.

Various residents were about at that early hour, but none paid any heed to the newcomers. Six tough-looking jaspers arriving together might easily have drawn unwelcome attention. Following the failure of the Lander job, Cain had resourcefully foreseen this possible dilemma.

Accompanied by the new recruit, he was the last to arrive. He paused in the middle of the street. A languid yet all-seeing eye casually panned the immediate vicinity. All was as it should be. He lifted his hat to wipe the sweat off his brow. That was the signal for all six outlaws to assemble behind the bank.

Unhurriedly yet with purpose, they strolled across leading their horses through the entrance giving access to the rear. Surprisingly, the gates were unlocked. This manager must either be full of confidence, or plain incompetent. He had clearly never faced a hardened band of robbers before. A fact that was hugely in their favour.

As expected the back door to the main building was locked. But Judge Fitzroy had somehow managed to secure a master key that could open most doors. Cain sucked in his breath when he inserted it into the lock. A momentary hesitation, then he turned it. The soft click of shifting levers brought a tight smile to his face.

'OK boys, this is it,' he hissed out quietly. 'According to my information, the cash office is on the first storey. There should be about four tellers in there, bagging up the dough ready for shipment to the head office in Casper.' All this had been discussed beforehand, but it didn't do any harm to issue a reminder before the actual attack. He pushed open the door. 'We hit them hard and fast then get out of there pronto. There shouldn't be any need for gunplay. Let's go.'

The six men hustled along a corridor to the stairs at the far end. In single file they went up, turning right at the top towards a room with a sign above the door announcing COUNTING OFFICE in bold capital letters. They tiptoed along the corridor to the door and listened carefully. The muted sound of voices could be heard on the far side.

Hand on the door knob, Cain breathed deep then pushed hard. In the shake of a dog's tail, the gang were inside. 'Hands up!' Cain shouted out. 'This is a heist. Don't nobody move.'

The room was bare apart from four desks, behind which the cashiers were assiduously writing up a tally of all the receipts. The money had already been counted and was stacked in the vault ready for shipment. The manager was arranging it into thousand-dollar packages, each labelled and wrapped in brown paper stamped with the bank's name.

Cain had been informed that the specially reinforced wagon accompanied by four guards would arrive around nine o'clock in the morning. A quick glance at the large clock on the wall told him it was 8.37 precisely, more than enough time to purloin the money and escape.

Such was the unexpected nature of the attack that the tellers were taken completely by surprise. Hands lifted to the ceiling as the gang spread out, keeping them covered with cocked revolvers. As expected, the door of the heavy iron vault was open. Cain immediately eyeballed the manager, a short, plump dude with eye-glasses perched on the end of a pudgy snout.

'You!' he rapped out. 'Fill these sacks with dough. And be quick about it.' The burbling manager's mouth vacillated like a landed trout gasping for air. His muscles failed to react, such was the harsh shock to the guy's nervous system. 'Move it, mister, if'n you don't want a gutful of lead.' He violently pushed the quivering jelly over to the back of the vault.

'Don't shoot,' croaked the terrified official. 'I'll do as you say.'

But he was all fingers and thumbs and kept dropping the sack. 'Hurry it up, can't you?' rasped the tetchy gang leader. 'We ain't got all day.' He turned to Abel. 'Keep an eye on the corridor. Anybody comes up herd 'em in here.'

The delay in filling the sacks had tempted a young teller to make a show of resistance. Abner Riverton peered around to make sure none of the robbers were watching. Here was his chance to make a name for himself. The young man had always harboured a dream of being a fearless town marshal. Preventing a hold-up would do his standing with the local girls no harm either.

Girding up his nerve, the cashier's right hand shifted towards an open drawer inside which was a small pistol. His hand settled over the gun. As he raised it, Dan Spurlock chose that moment to turn around and witness the surreptitious move.

His gun barked twice. The first shot was accurately

placed to blast the shooter out of the guy's hand without injuring him. It was immediately followed by the crash of breaking glass from the second bullet as the clock on the wall disintegrated. Riverton cried out and fell down, clutching at his numbed hand. He clearly had not given any thought to the perils of such a reckless manoeuvre.

Those shots were the last thing Cain Vender wanted. He cursed aloud. 'Thunderation!' he yelled out. 'We'll have the whole town after us now. Grab what you can boys and let's beat it.'

Another couple of shots above the tellers' heads sent them sprawling onto the floor as the gang quickly backed out of the room. A man alerted by the gunfire emerged from an adjoining room.

'What's happening here?' he yelped out. 'Who fired those shots?' On seeing the array of hoglegs aimed in his direction, the guy's hands shot up.

'We did, mister, and the next slug will be in your belly if'n you don't close that door.' Cain waved his revolver in the terrified guy's face. It was enough to see him disappearing faster than a scalded cat. The exit from the building was achieved at an equally swift rate.

Already shouts could be heard from the front of the bank as people congregated outside, wondering what all the commotion was about at such an early hour. By making use of the back entrance, the gang did not meet any opposition as they mounted up and galloped out of the gates. Following Cain's lead, the rest of the gang swung their horses between an untidy amalgam of shacks and back lots until they reached open country.

Once clear of the Granger town limits and safe from pursuit, Cain instructed his men to split up. 'Make your way back to the ranch by different routes boys, just like we planned. We'll meet up with the judge and his pals in a couple of days to divide up the take at my place.' He was pretty sure that any pursuit would be badly co-ordinated. Somehow, the gang's three Rock Springs associates had connived to send the marshal of Granger out of town on a wild goose chase.

When the gang broke up and went their different ways, Spurlock made certain to stick with Cain. It was ten minutes later that the gang leader drew to a halt, allowing his shadow to catch up. 'Didn't you hear what I said? We split up and meet at the ranch later?'

'I ain't familiar with this country like you,' Spurlock pointed out. 'And in any case I intend sticking to you like glue.'

'What's your beef, mister? Don't you trust me?'

'Not when your toting all that dough,' Spurlock countered. 'How do I know you won't make a run for it? All them lovely greenbacks must be mighty tempting.'

Cain huffed and puffed, angry at being accused of such a lowdown act of treachery. 'I wouldn't leave my own kin with nothing in the kitty. That ain't the Vender way. We stick together through thick and thin.' In an instant his hand was filled with hard metal. A fiery regard vehemently informed the new guy that any further insinuations would be bad for his health.

Spurlock held up a conciliatory hand. 'I ain't

accusing you of anything, boss. Just saying what some more suspicious fella might think.'

'Well now you know,' came back the brusque retort. 'Guys that stick with me and do their job are well rewarded.' He was still none too pleased at the company he was now forced to keep. But there didn't appear to be any option but to tolerate this new guy's presence.

The meandering trail back to the ranch continued for a spell in silence. Cain's frosty manner thawed somewhat once he had accepted that Spurlock was here to stay. 'Well, seeing as how we're gonna be partners for the next couple of days, you can tell me what it's like being a big-shot train robber.'

His tone was verging on the cynical, but in truth he secretly harboured a jealous streak. More than anything Cain Vender wanted to move into the big time. And this guy could provide him with a vital rundown on the techniques that had turned gangs like the Renos and the James Boys into household names. He'd heard of Cracker Dan Spurlock and his penchant for dynamiting reluctant safes. Fitzroy had checked up and found out he had amassed a notorious reputation west of the Pecos in New Mexico.

Drew Henry was now more than ever glad that he had learnt as much as possible about the real Spurlock prior to setting out on his mission of vengeance. Over the next twenty-four hours he had Cain Vender drooling at the mouth with envy as he described Spurlock's illicit exploits. The truth was substantially embellished to further enhance his credentials.

ELEVEN

BAD NEWS FOR CAIN

The six members of the outlaw gang, together with Judge Fitzroy and his cronies, were assembled in the living room of the Vender household. On the table were spread out the full takings of the Granger robbery. As the man most adept with figures, Elmer Hyde had been appointed as the duly authorized cashier.

Home-made moonshine, Hog's speciality, was being liberally consumed. Hog was also availing himself of the cookies and cherry cake baked by Ruth.

Spurlock was relieved to find the girl was nowhere to be seen. She had clearly made herself scarce, not wishing to be associated with the illicit distribution. The last thing he needed was to come face to face with her after his unintentional absence from the dance. He had a great deal of humble pie to consume if he was to ever redeem himself in her eyes.

'So how much of a share do we get?' pressed Judge Fitzroy, his beady peepers glittering with avarice as the green bank notes were distributed into their appropriate piles. All that dough sitting on the table was making him edgy.

As the self-proclaimed ringleader of the conclave, in the beginning of their association Fitzroy had tried to claim a larger share of any proceeds. This had been avidly opposed by his two associates, who reckoned their contributions were of equal worth. They had, however, come to an agreement between themselves that amounted to a larger share than the gang.

When the decision had been announced, Cain had hit the roof. Only the swift intervention of brother Hog had prevented blood being spilled. 'You bunch of conniving misfits must be nuts if'n you think we're gonna take all the risks for a lower cut. Far as I'm concerned it's equal shares for everybody. Including Biggs and Robey. Now take it or leave it. That's the deal.' The other gang members enthusiastically backed his play, especially the two henchmen who had never expected to be treated on an equal footing to the Vender boys.

It had been a tense stand-off, touch and go whether the scam proposed by Fitzroy would come to fruition. In the end, it was thought better to have a firm agreement than be constantly at loggerheads regarding the share-out.

So here they were once again with numerous successful jobs behind them, sitting at the same dining table eyeing the piles of banknotes expectantly. At long last, the prosecutor sat back. He was ready to reveal each man's cut. And the vinegary look on his face did not bode well.

'How much do we get?' snapped Cain acidly.

'It sure ain't what we were told to expect,' bristled the prosecutor. 'The take should have been much more than this. We had it on good authority that there would be at least forty big ones in that vault.'

Abel, the hot-headed member of the family, lunged at Hyde grabbing at his coat. 'Less mouthing off, Mr Prosecutor,' he growled. 'How much? That's all we want to know.'

Hyde shook himself free. 'No need for any of the rough stuff,' he remonstrated with some vigour, knowing he had the sheriff to protect him should things get over-heated. 'You guys have bungled the job yet again. It's only two thousand each. At this rate we ain't never going to enjoy the bright lights of San Francisco.'

That was the moment Dan Spurlock decided to intervene. 'The prosecutor is right. It's chicken feed. Your brother Sam could make more on his farm.' It was a blatant exaggeration but solidly rammed home his trenchant allegation.

Cain snarled out a rabid curse. 'It was all your damned fault. Shooting that teller was a crazy stunt. We were forced to leave before the job was finished.'

Normally a placid guy not prone to flashes of quick temper, Spurlock sensed that a more impassioned response was called for. He banged a fist on the table.

The glasses rattled. Even Hog took notice, his fourth piece of cake hovering betwixt the plate and an open maw.

'It's you that didn't organize things properly.' A caustic eye was fixed on the gang leader. A prodding finger backed up his accusation. 'You're a liability, mister.'

Cain leapt to his feet, his hand hovering above his gun. 'So you don't like the way I run things around here, eh?' was his acidic rejoinder. 'And I suppose you could have done a sight better?'

'You're darned tooting I could,' Spurlock declared lounging in his chair, completely unruffled by the imminent threat to his continued existence. 'First off, you ought to have had those dudes on the floor, every damned one of them, where they couldn't do no harm. And walking in there without masks gave them all a good look at our faces. Pen drawings will be plastered on dodgers scattered across the territory within a couple of weeks. The only thing you did right was to arrive separately.'

He turned to address the three officials. 'If'n you guys think I'm going in with these turkeys to rob a well-guarded train of one hundred grand then you're pissing into the wind.' He stood up and grabbed his share of the loot. 'A bunch of amateurs. That's all you are. Pah!!'

Turning to leave, an arm shot out to prevent his abrupt departure. 'Hang on there, fella. Let's not be too hasty.' Judge Fitzroy gently guided him back to his seat. 'Ain't no sense in us all falling out over this,' he iterated, trying to placate rising tempers. 'I'm sure we can work something out. A hundred grand sure ain't to be sniffed at.' He paused eyeing each man in turn, as if they were wayward members of his court. A particularly hard glare was reserved for Cain before he added with meaningful deliberation, 'Now is it, boys?'

Mutterings and twitchy looks saw the participants reluctantly settling back down to hear what the judge had to say. His next remark was aimed at the new man. And it was not what Cain Vender was expecting. Nor what he wanted to hear.

'Is that informant of your'n still ready to spill the beans on this large shipment you told us about?' A brisk nod found the judge continuing, 'So what if'n we were to put you in charge of this caper? Would that change your mind about quitting?'

'You can't do that,' Cain blurted out angrily, once again jumping to his feet. 'I'm the boss of this gang. We've done all right so far. It should be me running things.'

But the judge was adamant. And his two associates were equally forthright in their support. They had clearly been talking this over prior to arriving at the ranch.

'Sure, Cain, you've done OK,' Elmer Hyde insisted, pushing his twitchy snout forward to emphasize his next point. 'But these last couple of jobs prove you're losing your touch. Added to that you have no experience of robbing trains, whereas Dan here is clearly successful in that field.'

The prosecutor paused to allow the significance of his intimation to sink in. The use of Spurlock's first name had unmistakeably shifted allegiance away from Cain Vender to the sinister newcomer. That said, he did not want to alienate the gang leader. They still needed him and his men. So he quickly added, 'What the judge is suggesting is that Dan only runs this particular show. Ain't that right?'

Fitzroy nodded, hurrying on to placate the bristling attitude of the regular gang leader. 'That's right. It's just for this one job, if'n Dan is in agreement, of course.'

Spurlock's whole body tensed up. He gave a curt grunt of assent, being well aware that the next couple of minutes would determine his future. Yet not a flicker of uncertainty showed on his face. Confidence oozed from every pore, even though inside he was a quivering jelly. A stogie was lit up to calm his jangled nerves.

This was exactly as he had hoped the conflab would progress. But it could easily disintegrate into a violent gun battle should Cain turn nasty. It was Abel who unwittingly came riding to the rescue. 'He's right, brother, we don't know a goddamned thing about robbing trains. We need this guy, and his informant, to pull it off without any hitches.'

Hog also took up the cause in support of the temporary change of control. 'As the judge said, it'll only be this one time, Cain. With all that dough coming our way, we can up sticks and start again some place else if'n that's what you want.'

All eyes focussed on the prickly leader of the clan. Cain was none too pleased at having his position usurped. He rose to his feet and stumped around, a dour expression boding ill for anybody who interrupted his cogitations. Eventually after what seemed a long hour, in effect merely two minutes, he settled down. 'All right, I agree. Spurlock calls the shots. But only for the organization of the train side of things. I'm still in charge of the grab once the train has been halted.'

He looked to Spurlock for his agreement. 'I'm OK with that,' the newly elected leader said, puffing out a couple of smoke rings.

That announcement felt like the steam from a boiling kettle had been released. A collective sigh of relief issued around the room as muscles eased and men relaxed.

Sheriff Speakman was the first to break the silence. He splashed fresh liquor into their glasses. 'Let's all raise a toast to a successful job,' he proposed.

'The biggest we've ever pulled,' came the animated corollary from Abel Vender.

All present avidly concurred. Even Cain Vender appeared to accept the temporary secession of command. His face twisted into something akin to a tolerance of the general ruling.

'So how are we going to run this, Cracker?' Fitzroy enquired once the initial euphoria had dissipated. 'What do you have in mind?'

'First thing is for me to make contact with my

informant and arrange a date, time and place. That might take a few days. Once I have that information, I'll set up a meeting and we can go from there.' He stood up and stretched the stiffness from his muscles. 'It's been a hard few days, gents. Reckon I'll head back to the cabin and catch up on some shut-eye.'

He turned for the door, not forgetting to pocket his share of the Granger job. Although he was adamant in his mind that all this dough would eventually be returned to its rightful owners.

Once the guy had departed, daggers of hate from Cain Vender were aimed at the door. 'That guy ain't gonna get away with showing me up like that. I'll kill the skunk when this is over.'

Fitzroy was on his feet in an instant. 'You make darned certain to go along with what he says, Cain. This ain't no time for a vigilante reprisal. What you do after we've lifted the dough is no concern of mine.'

Outside it was already dark. Spurlock ambled across to the chestnut. A satisfied smile graced the handsome profile. Before he had time to mount up, a mordant voice cut in on his thoughts. It was Ruth Vender.

'So that's where you went last Saturday. I heard everything through the window. All night I waited at the Flying V hoping you would turn up. Do you know how humiliating that felt? Standing around while all the others were enjoying themselves. And all the time you were planning a bank robbery with them.' Her voice quivered with emotion as she slung a thumb behind.

'They only told me at the last minute that I was to

be included,' he offered feebly, trying to wriggle off the hook. 'If'n I'd known about it earlier …'

Ruth hawked out a disgusted snort of derision. 'It's too late for trotting out any lame excuses now. You're no better than Cain and the others.' Her accusation was scathing, sharp as vinegar. 'In fact you're worse, hiding behind a bunch of lies. At least my brothers don't claim to be anything other than what they are. But you …' She turned away to hide her anguish.

'I'm sorry you had to find out the hard way, Ruth.'

'Miss Vender to you. Only my friends and those I can trust are entitled to be personal,' she shot back. 'And you, Mr Cracker Dan Spurlock, are neither.' There were tears in her eyes. 'I thought you were different. A man I could respect, maybe even …' She stopped, unable to bring herself to say that special word.

The object of such bitterness longed to take her in his arms and tell her he was only play-acting. But that could never be. The lump in his throat almost made him choke on the deception he was forced to play. 'It's as well you learned the truth now rather than later … Miss Vender. That's the way it is. So I'll bid you goodnight.'

And with a heavy heart he mounted up and rode away, leaving the girl struggling desperately to contain the burning ache inside.

It was four days after that crucial meeting at the Vender ranch. The three conniving officials along with their newly appointed heist man were gathered in Elmer Hyde's law office which was tucked away down a side street. An impressive collection of law books lined the numerous shelves with authentic looking certificates filling in spaces on the walls; all designed to give the place an aura of competence and trust. Anybody seeking legal redress here would have been reassured that their case would be efficiently handled.

Spurlock struggled to contain his disapprobation.

He had wired Colonel Thruxton to meet on the far side of the Tabernacle Mountains in Rawlins, a halfway point between Laramie and Rock Springs. There, a full explanation of the plan he had in mind was laid out. The BAD Agency's director had wholeheartedly agreed. And together they had thrashed out a coherent means of achieving the desired end, namely the capture and eradication of the Vender Gang.

'I received this earlier,' Spurlock announced, handing over an official railroad delivery note to Judge Fitzroy. He didn't say anything else while the devious gavel smacker read it through.

'What does it say?' asked Elmer Hyde impatiently.

'Read it for yourself,' the judge snorted, passing the note across. 'Don't mean nothing to me.'

Hyde read it out aloud.

Message for Charles Dixon, Supervisor
The Greenstreet Grain Storage Company has deliv-
ered one hundred bushels of wheat to the rail depot
at Cheyenne for despatch on the morning train,

Wednesday the 16 July. You can take delivery at Flat Stone, estimated time of arrival, 1.53pm. Goods in leading wagon. Signed – Handling Superintendent.

Both Hyde and Speakman were as baffled as the judge. 'You better not be playing tricks on us, mister,' threatened the lawman acidly. 'What's this all about?'

'Did you guys think my contact would send out a message as good as announcing to everybody whose hands it passed through that a robbery was being planned?' He hawked out a mocking grumble of derision. 'He has more sense than that.'

'Then you'd better explain,' said Hyde.

'The message is for me – CDS, Cracker Dan Spurlock. Greenstreet refers to greenbacks and one hundred thousand being sent on that train on the date stated. Flat Stone is fictitious. You fellas heard of Table Rock?' Nods all around. Mention of the large haul had all three ogling the note. 'That's where we hold up the train. And the dough is in the leading car behind the loco and tender. Simple really. But who would ever suspect the true meaning?'

Speakman shook his head. 'I gotta hand it to you, Spurlock. You sure have the edge on those Vender brothers. I'd never have connected that note with its true implication.'

'The Venders done all right on small scale jobs,' Spurlock conceded. 'But they should leave the big stuff to guys that can handle it.'

'Have you figured out how to pull it off?' asked the

avaricious prosecutor whose tongue was hanging out like a slavering mutt. 'The 16th is only four days off. It don't give you much time.'

'We can always postpone it. But the next delivery won't be for some time. And it might not be for as much as this one.' Spurlock gave a casual shrug of the shoulders. 'It's your call.'

Furtive looks passing between the three men were followed by quick nods. Greed had gotten the better of them. Not to mention the uncertainty posed by a delay. 'If'n you're confident of doing the business, we're in agreement for you to go ahead.'

'Then here's how we organize it. I'll join the train at Medicine Bow Junction where it'll take on wood. When it nears Table Rock, that's when the action really starts.' He went on to explain in detail what his three associates needed to do.

'I won't have time to go see the Venders. It'll take me a couple of days to reach the junction. So it's up to you guys to pass on details of where they have to gather.' His final remark was vital to the success of the mission. 'And remember that there won't be time to fleece the passengers. Only when the train has come to a stop and the strong box removed should they reveal themselves.'

'Don't worry,' spluttered out a thoroughly animated Judge Fitzroy. 'We'll see they don't make a mess of it this time.'

TWELVE

SETTING THE TRAP

Drew Henry had arranged to meet up with Colonel Thruxton at the town of Rawlins. The BAD chief had booked a room in the National Hotel. He was accompanied by a Wyoming town marshal whom he introduced as Brickfist Ty Fagan. The steely-eyed lawman stood three inches taller than Henry, who was himself over six feet in height. The guy was a man mountain. And he looked the part too. Scars criss-crossed a once-handsome visage from all the fights he had broken up with his bare fists.

'Ty here is currently marshal of Lander in Freemont County,' Thruxton said, introducing the two men. 'I brought him in because he prevented the Venders robbing the bank there.' The chief paused before adding in a more subdued tone, 'That was the job that led to your brother's cover being exposed. So you both have good reason for wanting these critters brought to justice.'

They shook hands. Drew felt like his hand was being crushed to a pulp. With the greatest effort he somehow maintained a smile with gritted teeth. There was no animosity intended. Fagan took his brawny strength for granted.

When his mangled paw was eventually released, Drew quietly flexed it back to life while welcoming the legendary town-tamer. His single-minded subjugation of Thermopolis as the town's first official law officer once the vigilance committees had been disbanded was legendary.

Numerous other successful tamings had followed. As indicated by his nickname, Brickfist rarely needed to use his guns.

Drew had certainly heard of the famous lawman. But this was their first meeting. 'It's an honour to be working with such a legend,' he averred with genuine approbation. 'Your fame has gone before you.'

The guy seemed embarrassed by the acclaim he was receiving. 'Just doing my job is all,' he said, shuffling his feet awkwardly. 'Sometimes I don't know my own strength.' Drew could believe it. His hand still ached. 'It's led to a few broken bones along the way. But I ain't come out of those brawls unscathed as you can see.' A large mitt pointed to his gnarled kisser.

Thruxton took up the story. 'Ty here is only on loan from Freemont County. But if'n this job goes to plan I intend offering him a permanent job with the Agency. You two fellas working together should have no trouble clearing a bunch of owlhooters like the Venders. I've allocated ten regular deputies to assist him,' added Thruxton. 'I reckoned that should be enough including the two of you. They are all experienced gun hands. And I'll be going along as well.' Both agents turned as one in stunned surprise at this blunt announcement by their boss. 'I want to be in on the capture of these skunks. Cole was not only your brother. He was a valued member of the team. Sitting back in this office while you fellas put your lives on the line don't sit right.'

Drew eventually found his voice. He knew that he was speaking for Brickfist Fagan when he remonstrated with the older man. The colonel was no spring chicken. His thinning grey hair and spreading frame were ample cause to express reservations about his playing an active role in the forthcoming action.

'We both know you'd put your own life on the line to protect the men under your command, boss,' he emphasized. 'Ain't no denying that you did it in the war and have the honours to prove it. But that was a long time ago.'

'I'm not suggesting that I go rampaging around the territory chasing after these hoodlums,' Thruxton interjected with vigour. 'All I want is to be on hand when those Vender boys are taken. Naturally, you fellas will be doing all the hard work.' He chuckled loudly in an attempt to lighten the mood. 'I'll just accept all the accolades when we have them locked up.'

Drew tossed a raised eyebrow to his colleague.

When the boss had his mind set to something, nothing would sway him. 'What do you reckon, Ty?'

Fagan shrugged. 'Guess it's all right so long as you take a back seat. We're the one's who are paid to take risks, boss. You're the brains that runs the outfit. And that's just as important a job.'

Thruxton clapped his hands. He was like a kid on Christmas morning. It was an unusual sight to see their stern commander bristling with animated vitality. He hooked out a bottle of Scotch to toast the success of the imminent campaign. Over the drinks, the three men thrashed out the details of the trap to net the Vender Gang.

It was a couple of hours later that Drew Henry and Brickfist Fagan left the hotel to make their preparations. 'I sure hope the boss don't try muscling in on the action, Drew. He's too darned long in the tooth for stunts like that.'

'I'll be on the train with him,' Drew replied as they wandered down Rawlins' main drag. 'The old boy will be taking orders from me when the action starts. I'll make sure he keeps his head down if'n the bullets start flying.'

THIRTEEN

GUN BATTLE AT
TABLE ROCK

At the precise time designated in the advisory note now in the hands of Gideon Fitzroy, steam locomotive number 56 was trundling across the flats of the Great Divide Basin. A sprawling expanse of rolling terrain dominated by short grassy hillocks with the occasional upsurge of isolated rock clusters, Table Rock was one such intrusion. The Divide marked the separation between east and west of the continent as evidenced by the divergent flow of rivers.

This was the way pioneering wagon trains had come before the railroads made them obsolete. Some miles north of the current line, deep ruts etched a stark history of mass movement into the landscape. Thousands of optimistic settlers had passed this way in the 1840s bound for the Shangri La of Oregon. Independence Rock soared above the tremulous surge of the Sweetwater River onto which eager pioneers still carved their hopes and aspirations.

Three days' travel to the west lay South Pass, where a city had been established catering to the needs of immigrants at the halfway point of their three-month trek. The merging of the railroad at Promontory Point, Utah in 1869 effectively cut the journey time to Oregon substantially.

Drew Henry peered out of the express car window. His grandparents had come this way back 1847 to start a new life in Oregon's Willamette Valley. He had not visited them for a couple of years but regular correspondence assured him they harboured no regrets about undertaking the dangerous journey. Perhaps when this job was complete, he would head out that way. The hope that he would not travel alone was something only time and an intensely loyal young woman would have to determine.

'How far to Table Rock, brakeman?' he asked while checking his hardware.

'Another ten minutes and I'll be ready to uncouple,' he declared. 'Then it's all down to you guys.'

Drew nodded as they passed through a deep cutting. The mournful keening of the loco hooter brought a smile to his face. 'I didn't know we had Hank Wardle as the driver,' he said. 'That whistle ain't the same as the *Prairie Queen*. A bit more on the bubbly side. But you can tell Hank's style anywhere.'

'When he heard that we wanted a driver for a special to catch the Venders, he was the first to volunteer.'

This particular train was not on the regular schedule. It had been arranged by Colonel Thruxton for the specific task of capturing the Vender Gang. Number 56 was a spare loco hauling the express car up front with two passenger cars behind and a freight wagon at the rear. No genuine passengers were on the train.

Fagan and his men occupied the window seats on the side where the assailants would be waiting at the halt. A few extra non-combatant personnel had been commandeered to add credence to the legitimacy of the train. Cain Vender was no fool. Suspicions would immediately be raised if the cars appeared to be empty.

All too soon the moment of no return arrived. 'Time to get ready, Mr Henry,' the brakeman announced, opening the rear door and stepping outside.

'Well, this is it, Drew,' Colonel Thruxton averred, shaking his friend and colleague firmly by the hand. 'We're in your hands now.' The leader of the BAD guys had not changed his mind about coming along. No amount of arguing could persuade him to remain behind in the passenger car. He wanted to be in at the sharp end.

Both Drew and Ty Fagan had only concurred when the boss agreed to remain out of sight, and the firing line.

Drew followed the brakeman out onto the covered portico, watching as the guy leaned down with a big wrench to lever out the link rods. Uncoupling a moving train is no easy task. It was fortunate that this was an old car not yet fitted with the newly invented automatic knuckle coupler. With that in place the task would have been nigh impossible. Drew's heart was in his mouth as the brakeman sweated and strained, urgently wrestling to achieve the desired end.

Eventually, much to his relief the job was completed, and the passenger cars and wagon fell away behind. No words were spoken as Drew swung onto the connecting ladder and climbed up onto the roof of the car. Precariously balancing against the swaying motion of the train, he carefully made his way to the front end overlooking the loco and its tender of logs.

The drop was six feet. Not a great distance. But on a rocking train and with the landing on a mass of logs, it needed care to avoid a broken leg. A quick glance ahead revealed that Table Rock was about a half mile away. This had once been a regular halt to take on water prior to being superseded by the one at Medicine Bow. Now in a decrepit state of repair, the abandoned water tower had fallen onto its side.

Cain Vender and his gang would be in position close by so Drew needed to make his part in the operation appear like a genuine robbery. Judging the moment right, he leapt down immediately drawing his revolver. Once again his assumed persona had reverted to the guise of Cracker Dan Spurlock.

'OK, Hank, this is it,' he called out. 'Stop the train.'

The engineer turned and gave a brisk nod of understanding. Then he applied the brakes. The great iron beast shuddered as the shoes gripped the driving wheels. Squealing like a stuck pig, it gradually slowed, finally trundling to a halt exactly opposite the fallen tower. Whistling Hank had proved his worth.

Yet even before the locomotive had juddered to a stop, Spurlock had jumped to the ground. He was quickly joined by Cain Vender. The outlaw even had a smile creasing his hard features. 'Looks like you've come good, Spurlock,' he admitted, brandishing his own pistol. 'Can't say I didn't have my doubts.'

The two men hustled along to the express car and banged their gun butts on the door. 'Open up in there,' Cain growled out. 'This is a heist by the Vender Gang. Any delay and we'll blow this damned car to match wood.'

The rest of the gang were hidden further back from the track behind some rocks.

A raucous screech from the rollers and the door slid back. 'Throw your guns out, and don't try acting the hero, mister,' Cain spat out, waving his own revolver about. An old Navy Colt and a Springfield rifle hit the dirt. 'Now the strong box, then step back.' The brakeman did as he was told. Instantly Abel and Hog ran forward and manhandled the heavy box away from the train.

'I'll stay here and keep an eye on these jaspers,' Spurlock said.

But Cain was not listening. Greed had gotten the better of him. All eyes were now focussed on opening the box. Only half an eye was kept on the express car and loco engineer. The mesmeric strong box was like honey to a bee, luring the gang across to take a peek at all that dough.

Another few seconds and they would be distracted sufficiently for Spurlock to show his hand. He knew that Brickfist and his men would have left the abandoned freight car by now and should be in place somewhere close by. As soon as the gang opened the box, they would realize the planned robbery was nought but a trap. For it contained nothing but rocks.

He swung to face the preoccupied outlaws and was ready with the order to surrender. But at that very moment, Isaac Thruxton appeared in the open doorway. 'Lay down your arms. We have you skunks surrounded. You're all under arrest for armed robbery.'

As if by instinct, Cain swung on his heel and jerked off a couple of shots. Thruxton had inadvertently placed himself in an exposed position. His white shirt and light grey trousers made him a sitting target. The bullets were well placed and struck the detection agency leader in the chest. His gun slipped from nerveless fingers as he tumbled out of the train.

'It's a darned trap, boys,' the gang leader hollered out. 'That Judas has betrayed us. It's every man for himself now.'

The gang quickly took cover and began peppering the express car with lead. Spurlock dived behind the tower as bullets buzzed passed his ears. He replied with a couple of shots to make his presence felt and keep their heads down until Ty Fagan made their presence felt. And it better be soon.

A half-formed curse hissed from between gritted teeth at the impetuous reaction of his boss. Another minute and he would have had the whole gang at his mercy as they gathered round the strong box. Now the guy looked as if he would be joining those black-banded pictures on the wall of the office in Laramie.

Luckily the brakeman had more sense. A spare rifle poking out of the small window ably supported the lone outside defender.

'Looks like there's only Spurlock and the brake-man,' suggested Hog Vender. 'Why don't we rush them?'

Cain was less than enthusiastic. 'You gonna lead the charge, brother?' The query was loaded with sarcasm. 'We'll spread out and catch him that way. The critter ain't got eyes in the back of his head.'

He was about to give the order when a hail of lead chipped bark behind which he was sheltering. 'What in blue blazes…?' he yelped, swivelling round as more bullets were aimed in their direction. 'It's a posse. They must have been in those cars that were left down the line.'

Plug Yancy had eagerly joined the gang with the lure of a hefty slice of the pay-off. But he was no hero and quickly saw the writing was on the wall. He stood up, hurrying across to where the horses were tethered. But he never made it. Half a dozen chunks of lead cut him down. But Cain was not finished yet. 'Use your rifles to keep them at arm's length, boys. I'm going after that treacherous rat, Spurlock.' Making use of a depression in the ground, he crawled off to his left. While the object of Cain's wrath was occupied by Abel, the gang leader sneaked around the back of the train and climbed up onto the roof of the express car.

On hands and knees, he crept silently forward until he was overlooking the point where Spurlock was secreted down below. The BAD agent was completely oblivious to the danger he now faced. Peering over the edge, Cain's mouth split in a malevolent grin. His gun appeared ready to blast his nemesis into the hereafter.

But he had reckoned without the intervention of Hank Wardle. From his elevated position in the loco cab, the engineer had a perfect view of the bush-whacker. 'Look out behind you, mister!!' he hollered.

Spurlock's reaction was instinctive. He threw his body to one side as Vender's bullet chewed a hole in his jacket. A sharp sting told him that blood had been drawn. But luckily it was only a flesh wound. Lying prone on his back, he emptied his gun at the hovering outlaw. But there was only one bullet left, and it struck the stovepipe whining off like an angry hornet. Cain's head disappeared as he scrambled down the far side of the car.

The temporary lull allowed both men time to reload their revolvers. Spurlock peered beneath the car but he couldn't see which way the guy had gone. All he could hear was the scuffling of Cain's boots on the shingle.

'He's over this side,' hissed Wardle quietly so the outlaw would not overhear, 'beside the drive wheels. Looks like he's going round by the cowcatcher. If'n you make use of the cab to climb onto the boiler ledge, you'll be above him. There's plenty of cover behind the valve domes and smoke stack.'

Spurlock nodded his thanks, scrambling up onto the servicing shelf. Gun held at the ready, he moved along until he was behind the large balloon stack. A quick glance round and there was Cain Vender. Spurlock hauled himself up behind the stack and waited until Vender was rounding the cowcatcher. Then he called out, 'Drop your gun, Cain. This is the end of the line for you.'

The gang leader froze. Arms outstretched, he slowly began to turn around, the revolver still clutched in his hand. 'You're a mighty tricky dude, Spurlock. Or whatever your name is. I ought never to have trusted you. And I wouldn't have neither if'n that knucklehead of a judge hadn't stuck his nose in.'

'Drop the gun,' the hidden BAD guy repeated. 'This is your last warning. My men have your gang surrounded. You ain't going nowhere. And just for the record, my real name is …' He paused to draw out the impact of his next revelation. '… Drew Henry. It was my brother Cole you hanged in that barn.' The utterance crackled with undiluted hatred. 'And I'm going to make sure you pay the full price.'

A stunned silence followed as Cain Vender contemplated the significance of what he had stumbled into. 'You can try, mister. But Cain Vender don't scare easily.'

In the background, heavy gunfire told of a fierce

battle ensuing. And it wasn't all going according to plan. One of Fagan's deputies had been killed and another wounded. But the Vender Gang was outgunned and outmanned. Axell Robey and his buddy were trapped in a cluster of rocks with no way out. Their ammunition was running low.

It wasn't meant to be like this. According to Dan Spurlock it should have been a simple operation. So they hadn't brought any spare shells. And so it would have been had the guy not played them for suckers. Now the die was cast. As things stood they were stuck between a rock and a hard place.

'Stay here and we're done for,' Biggs intoned in a dejected mutter. It was a joyless finale occupying the thoughts of both men. 'What say we make a dash for the horses?'

'We could toss out our guns and surrender,' suggested Robey.

Biggs was sceptical. 'Don't forget their boss has been killed. Those dudes are good and mad. They might not want to take any prisoners. And what's the option if'n we do give up? At least a heavy spell in the can, or more likely a rope's end.'

'Guess you're right, pard,' replied Robey, letting fly the last of his bullets. 'That's me out of ammo.'

Tight smiles passed between the two old pals as they rose as one and made a spirited run across open ground to where the jittery mounts were tugging at their ties. Immediately they became exposed, a lethal salvo opened up. Frantically zig-zagging from side to side they made good progress. But it was only a temporary delay of the inevitable. Biggs was the first to go down.

Robey ignored his stricken partner and carried on. Bent low, he finally made it to the horses and desperately leapt up onto the saddle. Sharp spurs dug into the sorrel's flanks as he swung away from the source of the deadly fusillade.

And he almost made it. Bullets zipped and whined all around him tugging at his clothes. That was when the attackers found their range. Six rifle slugs struck him in the back. The victim threw up his arms and tumbled out of the saddle, dead before his riddled body hit the ground. A cheer went up from the posse.

'Now you can see what's gonna happen to any more of you turkeys that make a run for it,' threatened the booming caveat of Brickfist Ty Fagan. 'You'd be well advised to throw out your guns now. Any more resistance and you know what to expect. No prisoners, no trial. Think about it, boys. But don't be too long. I ain't a patient man.'

Following the deaths of the two henchmen, there was a lull in the fighting. Both factions now took stock of their situation, each from their respective positions.

'Time's up, boys,' Fagan called out. 'We're coming to get you.' A heavy fusillade of hot lead struck the rocks protecting the two outlaws, showering them with sharp fragments.

Abel and Hog Vender ducked down out of sight. They were both tough desperadoes, and loath to surrender. It was not in their nature. They knew what was waiting at the end of the line. But life is precious. And where there's life there's hope, however slim and tenuous that tread might be. Remain in their current situation and a violent death was just around the corner. That notion was enough to see Hog desperately waving a white handkerchief.

'OK, mister, you win,' he spluttered. 'Hold your fire. We're coming out.'

'Throw out your weapons and reach,' the BAD agent rapped. 'Any tricks and you're both buzzard bait.'

The Battle of Table Rock was almost over. Now only Cain Vender was left.

FOURTEEN

THE CHASE IS ON

Over by locomotive number 56, the separate confrontation was fast approaching its climax. But the outlaw boss was not going to give up as easily as his brothers. Cain had other ideas. And surrender was not one of them. He knew that a necktie party would be his only reward. Cole Henry, the brother of this Judas. The disclosure had certainly come as a shock. And he had stumbled right into the trap.

But the gang leader had not worked himself up to be the dominant force of lawless endeavour in Wyoming to meekly submit to a neck stretching.

'So that's what this is all about? A BAD guy sent to avenge another one. I'm the real bad guy around here, and I intend to stay that way,' he called out with assurance.

Straight away, Cain stepped briskly to his right, forcing Drew Henry to swivel round the cumbersome smoke stack to keep his adversary in view. That was where he came unstuck. His boot slipped on a patch of oil. Struggling to maintain his balance, Drew was forced to cling onto the body of the stack. A couple of bullets from Cain's revolver clanging against the metal kept his head down.

That momentary shift in fortune allowed the outlaw to dart away to where the dead Robey's horse was now grazing. Bullets from the posse pursued the fleeing outlaw as he urged the sorrel up to the gallop. But the range was too great and he managed to escape unharmed.

Drew slithered along the boiler-housing ledge desperate to get after the escaping killer of his brother. But he had no horse. Then from his loftier position, he noticed the ones abandoned by the gang. They were a good hundred yards away. But there was no other choice. Ty Fagan and his boys were still fully occupied securing the two surviving prisoners and tending their injured men.

Jumping down, Drew raced across to the remuda. A good luck toot from Hank Wardle's ebullient whistle was plucked away by a determination to run his quarry to earth. He chose the nearest horse, a bay mare saddled up and ready for the chase. Cain had headed off in a westerly direction. An initial thought was that he was heading back to the ranch, which was no doubt where his ill-gotten gains were stashed.

The fleeing villain's trail was quickly picked up. It was not difficult to follow. A stiff breeze had blown up, shredding the cloud bolls into streamers of white. The committed hunter tightened the chin strap of his hat. A billowing plume of dust some two miles ahead rose into the swirling air. The wind had done him a big favour. It told him the direction in which the guy was heading. And it looked as if his supposition had been correct.

Then another far more sobering thought occurred to the pursuer.

How would Ruth respond when she learned the truth? Ever since that first meeting in McVay's store, Drew Henry's role had been a complete charade. The wayward family she had struggled so hard to straighten out had been rent asunder. And it was all down to him.

But Drew's thoughts were for Ruth's safety. Cain would be desperate when he reached the ranch. There was no knowing how he would handle things. And desperate men are liable to go off half cocked. He could force Ruth to go with him, maybe even as a hostage – his life for hers if cornered.

Drew was torn by two conflicting emotions. Vengeance demanded that he utterly eradicate the gang that had caused his own brother's death. But how could that be achieved without ruining forever his relationship with the girl with whom he now realized he had fallen in love? It was an earth-shattering revelation. And one he had never thought to experience following the death of his beloved Gabby.

Reconciliation of the stark inconsistency was tearing at his soul. He rode on following the tell-tale signs left by the absconding fugitive. One thing was for sure. No matter what, Cain Vender could not be allowed to escape. He owed that stark fact to Cole's memory.

Drew's problem was that he was not gaining on the brigand. In fact, the skunk was drawing steadily further ahead. He cursed his luck for being saddled with a nag only fit for the glue factory. At this rate, the runaway was going to escape his just desserts. He was approaching the Tabernacle range of mountains on the far side of which was the Vender spread, when a soaring butte of red sandstone caught his attention.

Known as the Bodkin, Drew suddenly recalled from previous forays while running with the Starrbreakers that a little-used Indian trail branched off close by. The Venders were relatively new to the territory and might not be aware of the short cut through the mountains. The detour would save him a good two hours of travel. Enough time to lay an ambush for the unsuspecting fugitive.

Praying hard to a god he had ignored for too long, Drew Henry was rewarded by the distant sight of rising dust along the main highway. A huge sigh hissed from between puckered lips. His supposition had been correct. Cain had passed by the narrow trail, clearly unaware of its significance.

Drew swung by the soaring monolith and pushed onwards. He knew just the place to mount his ambush and catch the rat off guard. It was a shelf of flat rock some ten feet wide overlooking the track which Cain Vender had taken. Known as the Flat Iron, it was well named. Drew hid his cayuse behind the adjoining rocks. All he needed was a lariat together with the skill to effectively use it.

Time spent on the Circle K ranch with Frank Kendrick had made him no less than an expert roper. A smile was fixed to the hunter's hard-boiled façade as he scrambled up onto his perch to survey the back trail.

Five minutes later, the steady drub of hoof beats assailed his ears. He had only just made it. The coiled loop of twisted manilla was held loosely in the right hand as he crouched on the edge of the shelf, the other end of the forty-foot serpent gripped tightly in his left. A plinth of rock kept him hidden from view as the unsuspecting rider drew near some four feet below.

The coiled rope spun overhead as the rider trotted ever closer. Timing was all-important if the catch was to succeed. Drew allowed his quarry to pass before launching the spinning loop on its way. Immediately following its release, the thrower wrapped the free end around his arm. Stiffened heels dug firmly into a crack ready for the haul-back. Circling in the fetid air like a giant plate, the uncoiling noose winged towards its target.

The drop was timed to perfection. Arms pinioned to his chest, Cain Vender was dragged from the saddle. He landed with a bone-crunching jar on the hard ground. Once he knew that the outlaw was at his mercy, Drew scuttled back down the rough slope behind. He wanted to be out front before his victim could recover his wits.

But Cain Vender had not led a notorious gang of outlaws without being able to rapidly face and adapt to the unexpected. The sudden assault had taken him completely by surprise. A lesser guy would have been nonplussed. Not so Cain Vender. As Drew rounded the lower edge of the shelf, the outlaw had already shaken off the confining restraint of the lariat. He shook the mush from his head and staggered to his feet to face the bushwhacker.

'You're like the cat with nine lives, Judas,' he snapped out, hunching down into the classic gun-fighting stance. 'Well they've run out. It's just you and me now. So let's see who walks away.' A rabid snarl rumbled in his throat. 'And it ain't gonna be you. Now grab your piece and let's get this over with.'

Drew flexed his gun arm and his fingers. Being right handed, he was glad the lucky shot from Cain's gun on the boiler had sliced a chunk from his left arm. Unlike the scowling outlaw, Drew's bearing was relaxed, even blasé, as if he didn't care. It was a ploy to deceive his opponent. Tension in the arm slowed a man down. All he needed was a cool eye to sense when the other man was about to make his move. A lift of the shoulder, curling of the fingers, twitch of the mouth. Each man had his own quirky precursor to signal an imminent showdown.

On this occasion, Drew had a double-edged reason for wanting this guy strumming with the Devil. Not only his brother, but also a highly respected boss – the man he had regarded almost like a father – had been rubbed out by this snake in the grass. He shook off the rising tide of anger threatening to break his concentration. Personal animosity had to be erased from his mind.

Over on a clump of cholla cacti, a meadow lark twittered. The lyrical cadence was cut short as a hawk plunged down and scooped it up. The fracas was brief, feathers fluttering in the breeze the only reminder of how tenuous life is in this wild terrain. The same correlation likewise applied at the top end of the food chain.

'Ready when you are, buster,' Drew iterated with a disdainful sneer. A final jibe at a guy's courage was always enough to precipitate an immediate response. 'I ain't got all day. Ruth will be waiting for me.'

Cain's anger erupted in a slap of hand on leather as he palmed his revolver. He was fast. No doubt about it. The gun rose, the hammer snapped back. And a double roar of gunfire bounced off the surrounding rock wall. Drew felt a hot draught whistle past his left ear. But he was more than equal to the challenge. His own shot was accurately placed.

Cain staggered back a pace, reeling drunkenly as he clutched at the fatal chest wound. His mouth opened in surprise, blood dribbling from the open maw. 'Guess you must … have only used up … eight of them … lives.' They were his last words as he fell to the ground.

The taking of a man's life never came easy to Drew

Henry, even if it was a ruthless desperado like Cain Vender. Cracker Dan Spurlock had been returned to his grave. A cold shiver rippled through his sparse frame as the assumed persona was shed like the skin of a rattlesnake. Once again he could be himself.

Only one task was left to complete his mission. The nailing of those three odious specimens purporting to uphold the law while shamefully abusing their hallowed positions. Fitzroy, Hyde and Speakman had much to answer for. And it was Drew Henry who was going to nail their miserable hides to a barn door. He laughed out loud at the play on words. And hide as they might, he would hunt them down.

But then another task loomed large in his thoughts. One to which he was most definitely not looking forward – the inescapable confrontation with Ruth Vender. How would she react to him bringing in the dead body of her brother? The other two were in custody and likely to face a hangman's rope for their villainy. For the moment all he could do was shut out the prospect as he tied Cain's body across the saddle of his horse.

Once secured, it was with a heavy heart that he set off for the Vender ranch.

In the meantime, Ty Fagan had herded the prisoners back to the abandoned section of the train and locked them in the rear car along with the horses. He then rode back to the waiting locomotive. Before Whistling Hank reversed the train to recouple the two sections,

Fagan gently lifted the heavy body of Isaac Thruxton into the express car and reverently laid it down on a cot.

'The boys will see to it you receive a fitting send-off, Colonel,' the big man murmured with tears in his eyes. Although he had only known the BAD boss a short time, he knew the guy would be hard to replace.

One of Fagan's men, a guy whimsically called Squirrel Foot Kelly who was adept at handling a morse key, scrambled up a telegraph pole and tapped out a message back to the Agency's temporary base in Rawlins, signalling that the operation had been a success. No mention was made concerning the untimely death of their boss. That would need to be done by word of mouth.

Soon after, the train huffed and puffed back into motion heading up line to the next available turn-around facility some ten miles away at Greasy Grass Junction.

FIFTEEN

MIXED FORTUNES

Telegraph clerk Cleophas Dowd had been dozing in his office on the main street of Rock Springs when the message came through. It was from a colleague down the line in Rawlins. The news that was tapped out brought a wide-eyed gape from the bored official. He immediately sat up, assiduously scribbling down the momentous newsflash.

It read:

VENDER GANG AMBUSHED BY BAD AGENTS WHILE TRYING TO ROB TRAIN AT TABLE ROCK. ABEL AND ESAU CAPTURED. NOW IN RAWLINS JAIL AWAITING TRIAL. OTHER GANG MEMBERS KILLED. ONLY CAIN THEIR LEADER STILL AT LARGE. NOW BEING HUNTED DOWN BY AGENT DREW HENRY WHO INFILTRATED GANG. PRISONERS REVEALED THAT LEADING COUNTY OFFICIALS WERE THE RINGLEADERS. NAMES UNKNOWN.

Ripping the cable off the pad, the clerk rushed out of the office and over to the jailhouse to inform Sheriff Speakman. Rather than displaying elation at such good news, the blood drained from the lawman's face. Dowd was nonplussed at the unexpected reaction. The guy ought to have been jumping for joy. The county had been plagued by this gang for too long already.

'Something wrong, Sheriff?' he asked the gaping starpacker. 'Looks like you've seen a ghost.'

Speakman snapped out of his shocked demeanour. 'J-just s-surprised is all,' he stuttered out. 'A bit jealous that it wasn't me that captured those crooks.'

But Dowd was not convinced. He was even more suspicious when Speakman blurted out, 'Have you told anyone else yet?'

'No, I reckoned you should be the first to know.'

'Then make sure you don't spread it around,' rasped the sheriff before adding in a more conciliatory voice, 'Best if'n I tell the judge and let him decide how to announce the … erm … good tidings.'

'As you say, Sheriff,' Dowd muttered as he left the jailhouse. But he had no intention of keeping such tremendous news to himself. He hurried across the street into McVay's store. 'You guys will never guess what I've just been told.' There were half a dozen customers in the store as well as the proprietor and his son. All eyes swung to focus on the normally innocuous Cleophas Dowd as he babbled out the gist of the message, adding a few juicy extras to enhance the telling.

Judge Fitzroy and his partner in crime were

panic-stricken on hearing the news they had all been dreading. News like that could not be contained for long. Their activities within the county were already regarded by some of the more astute citizens with scepticism and even hostility. As leading members of the town council, bank manager Jasper Mawdsley and Elias McVay the storekeeper were already asking awkward questions.

'Reckon it's time to quit while we're ahead, boys,' Fitzroy declared. 'Those Vender boys have already squealed like stuck pigs. It's only a matter of time before our names come to light.'

The safe was quickly cleared and their ill-gotten gains shared out. 'There's enough here for us to start up elsewhere, some place west of the Tetons where the telegraph ain't reached.' Before he had even finished speaking, Fitzroy was heading for the back stairs of the courthouse.

But the three guilty officials were too late.

A crowd of angry men led by McVay blocked their escape. 'You fellas in a hurry?' McVay sneered, brandishing a Colt revolver. 'You wouldn't be thinking to make a run for it with all that dough you've stashed away, would you?' The measured query packed full of irony was accompanied by the more earthy growl of anger from the other members of the council.

'Of course not,' blustered Hyde. 'We were just coming to see you, Jasper, about those contracts you were preparing.'

The banker was not taken in by the shallow pretext.

He grabbed one of the saddle bags and delved inside. 'Well look what we have here,' he declared, lifting out a wedge of banknotes. 'I'm not usually a gambling man, but my bet is those other bags contain more of the same.' A hard edge took over as he snapped out an order to the more physical members of the council. 'Grab them, boys. Then march the skunks over to the jailhouse. You rats can see what it's like on the wrong side of the cell bars for a change.'

'You can't do this,' protested Tash Speakman, struggling as two brawny farmers disarmed him and laid heavy hands on his shoulders. 'I'm the law around here.'

'Not any more you ain't,' butted in Elias McVay. 'The days of you and that bunch of crooks running this town are over. Take them away, boys. We have a multiple hanging to organize.'

As the angry mob was crossing the street, manhandling the prisoners, Sam Vender was approaching on his wagon. The chicken farmer had chosen that day to make his weekly visit to Rock Springs for supplies. He had called at the ranch to pick up Ruth on the way. Neither of them had heard about the failure of their outlaw kinfolk to rob the train. The gang had been gone for three days.

As always when they rode off on one of their nefarious schemes, she had fretted constantly until their safe return. Much as she detested their lawless ways, Ruth harboured a forlorn expectation that she could one day convert them to a more honourable way of life.

Since the arrival of Dan Spurlock on the scene, the cool, practical side of her nature had been at loggerheads with her heart. Much as she had berated the charlatan for his odious deception, there was no denying that she had fallen under his spell. Conflicting messages surging through her distraught mind were becoming more than she could bear.

Such inconsistent thoughts were rampaging around inside her head when a shout went up. 'There's another of those bandits! Get him, boys, before he escapes.'

Before the pair knew what was happening, Sam Vender had been dragged from the wagon. Numerous stray fists made it patently clear that the farmer's blameless character counted for nothing. He had been tarred with the same brush as his lawless brothers. Ruth was pushed to one side, being regarded as an innocent victim of their heinous actions.

Much as she tried remonstrating with the incensed mob, her pleas fell on deaf ears. It was with a heavy heart that Ruth Vender returned to the ranch alone. And that was where she found Dan Spurlock waiting on the veranda. But it was the body draped across a horse that caught her attention. Leaping off the wagon, she hurried across. A cry of anguish burst forth on witnessing the blood-stained corpse of her elder brother. Ruth sank to her knees. Head in hands, the tears flowed like rain.

Drew Henry had a burning desire to rush across and hold her in his arms, to whisper comforting endearments in her ear. But he held back. How would she react? Fall into his arms, or push him away as the man who destroyed her family? It was Ruth who finally took the initiative.

She looked across at the solitary figure. Tall and handsome, his warm, endearing nature tugged at her heart strings. The tune it played was one of love and longing. A yearning for normality with this man by her side.

'I don't blame you for what's happened, Dan,' she murmured, barely above a whisper. 'This was always going to be the finale for the Vender brothers. I was burying my head in the sand thinking I could change them.'

All the tension that had built up since that final shoot-out at the Flat Iron drained away. He ran across. Pausing for a moment to ensure he had not read the signs wrong, he waited. It was Ruth who stood up and fell into his arms. A shudder of rapture coursed through the entwined bodies. They kissed. It was soft and yielding. A smouldering passion threatened to encompass them both. But the recent grim events forced them apart.

'You best stop calling me Dan,' the star-struck guy declared as he came up for air. 'My real name is Drew Henry. Cracker Dan Spurlock was a train robber operating in New Mexico who met his end in a prison fight. Maybe we should go inside and I can tell you the whole story.'

Ruth's eyes widened. 'Then you must have been related to the man who was hanged.'

Drew nodded. 'He was my brother.'

The girl bowed her head in shame. 'That was down to my brothers. How I could have stayed on knowing the bad things they were engaged in is mortifying. Their guilt is on my hands. How can you ever forgive me?'

'You were only trying to help them steer a legitimate course,' Drew assured her. 'I don't blame you. They chose to ride the owlhooter trail. And they've paid the price.'

Arm in arm they strolled across to the house while Drew outlined what had occurred at Table Rock and its aftermath.

That was the moment the dream of a settled life with Ruth Vender found itself teetering on the edge of a dark abyss.

SIXTEEN

VIGILANTE LAW

'But it isn't over yet, Drew!' Ruth exclaimed, wringing her hands as a despairing turmoil gripped her very essence.

Perplexity showed on her paramour's face. 'What do you mean? Has something happened?'

'The town has gone crazy,' she blurted. 'They must have somehow learned about the robbery and that my brothers were involved. They arrested the judge and his associates. Then they saw Sam and me coming down the main street and arrested him. But Sam has never been involved with their dealings. He always condemned them and wanted me to go live with him.'

'He told me all about it just before the robbery,' Drew admitted.

'We have to save him.' Ruth was now frantic with worry. 'McVay is whipping the town up into a frenzy of hate against those critters. They're mad enough to do anything. And Sam will get the same treatment. I'm scared, Drew.'

He held her tightly. 'Don't fret none, honey. I'll ride like the devil back to Rock Springs and make sure those guys don't do something they'll regret. There's no place in Wyoming for vigilante law. You stay here,' he added. 'The way things stand at the moment, that town is no place for a woman, especially one called Vender. I'll take a fresh horse. Mine is done for.' He did not stop to argue. Within minutes, he was mounted up and urging the cayuse to the gallop.

The main street of Rock Springs was deserted when he arrived. A raucous din was coming from inside the Big Horn saloon. And it sounded like the good citizens were girding themselves up for a hanging. Drew had been involved in vigilante trials before. It was an ugly sight he did not want repeated and one of the reasons he became a BAD boy.

He quickly dismounted outside the sheriff's office and hustled inside. Angus McVay was wearing a badge commandeered from Tash Speakman. 'What do you want, mister? Nobody is allowed in here without permission from the committee.' His hand reached for the gun on his hip.

He was no match for a BAD agent. 'Don't be a fool, kid. You're out of your depth in this fracas. Now give me that badge. As an authorized special agent I'm assuming the rank of sheriff until a proper election can be held.' He held out his hand. The revolver clutched in his meaty fist did not give the unfortunate kid much choice.

Drew pinned the tin star to his jacket. 'Now you can join me outside to quell the lynch mob that will be here soon. Or join those critters in the cell block. Your choice, fella. But I ain't got no time for dallying.' His ears pricked up. 'Hear that? Sounds like they've made their decision. And it sure ain't an invitation to a tea party.'

'OK, I'll back you up,' said Angus McVay. 'I was never in favour of taking the law into our own hands when Pa suggested we hold a trial in the saloon.'

Drew grabbed one of the shotguns standing in a rack on the wall. 'You take the other one, Angus. And stand to one side when we step outside. That way we'll offer a smaller target if'n some clown decides to push his luck.' He fixed the boy with a stern look. 'You can use one of these scatter guns, can't you?'

'Of course I can,' scoffed the demoted sheriff.

In truth he had never held one in his life before today. And he prayed silently that he would not be called upon to use it.

'You ready for this, partner?'

The young man squared his shoulders. Partnering a tough hombre like this guy, life couldn't get any better. In the past, Angus had always succumbed to his domineering father. Well those days were gone. Now it was his chance to demonstrate there was a measure of hard steel in his backbone. 'Never more so. Let's go stop us a lynching.'

Drew couldn't help smiling at the kid's bravado. He

only hoped he would not buckle under the pressure from a blood-crazed mob. The way he was holding that Loomis didn't exactly fill him with confidence.

'Hey, boy, you in there?' It was Elias McVay. The slurred drawl indicated that the mob's leader had been enjoying a liberal slurp of the hard stuff. 'Time to bring out those four critters. The tribunal has passed a unanimous verdict of guilty. It's the hanging tree for the conniving no-goods.'

Angus stepped out onto the veranda, the shotgun cradled in his arms. His father was at the front of a considerable gathering of the town's citizens. He was flanked by Jasper Mawdsley and Cleophas Dowd. The latter was holding a hemp noose in readiness for the main attraction. Those behind were jostling for position. Nobody was expecting any glitches, far less trouble from a weak-kneed kid like Angus McVay. It was something of a shock, therefore, to see the store clerk brandishing a lethal scatter gun.

'Watch where you're pointing that thing, Angus,' heckled one wit at the back. 'It might go off.' Numerous guffaws followed this ribald comment.

'OK, boy, you've had your moment of glory,' his father bristled. 'Now bring the scum out or we'll go in and get them.'

'No you won't,' rapped out a low voice but one that was impossible to ignore as Drew Henry stepped out to join his partner. 'There ain't going to be any hangings in Rock Springs unless a lawful verdict has been passed in an authorized court of law.'

'It's that turkey who was hanging out with the Venders,' shouted another bystander. 'Let's add him to the swingers.' A roar of approval went up as those at the rear pushed forward.

'Stand back!' Drew rapped out, aiming the shotgun directly at Elias McVay. 'I'm the sheriff now. Any man who disagrees can argue with my friend here.' He tapped the stock of the shotgun. 'There'll be no vigilante law here nor anyplace else in Wyoming. And you have that assurance from an accredited special agent of the BAD organization. Drew Henry at your service, gents. So what's it to be?'

'He's bluffing, grab him, boys, and let's get this over with.' The blatant challenge had come from somebody protected by the crowd.

The telegraph clerk took this as a signal for action. He stepped forward, his foot on the boardwalk. But that was as far as he got. Drew swung the butt of the shotgun across his head. The guy never knew what hit him. He hit the dirt like a sack of potatoes. 'Anybody else tries a stunt like that, he's in big trouble. Give this bunch of lunatics a taste of what they can expect, deputy.' Drew fervently hoped that young McVay would aim high and not into the crowd. The last thing he needed was blood on his hands at this stage of the negotiations.

But he need not have feared. The alleged milksop had grown up fast. One barrel of the Loomis blasted out its death-dealing charge of buckshot, shredding the Long Horn signboard to splinters. A fresh cartridge was instantly slotted into the empty barrel, the gun swinging to cover the crowd. 'The next shot won't be so high,' he snarled out, weaving his lip into a suitably aggressive curl.

Drew's face split into a menacing grin of accord. 'The show's over, folks, go about your business before anybody gets seriously hurt. And take this idiot with you.'

The two lawmen clearly meant business. Suddenly all the bluster and false daring fizzled out. Nobody was ready to place their life on the line for a few bad apples. The proper courts could deal with them. The crowd slowly dispersed, including Elias McVay, who was eyeing his son in a completely different light. Respect, even admiration, showed in his face.

'You done well, boy.'

The two unofficial lawmen waited unmoving until the street was clear before returning to the office. The door had not even closed when Ruth Vender hurried in and threw her arms around Drew. 'I couldn't stay home,' she elicited. 'Not with you putting your life in danger to save Sam.'

'Then you'd better release him,' Drew said. 'But make sure it's only him who walks free. Those other turkeys will be tried and sentenced in the proper manner.'

'Do you think we can ever put all this behind us?' she purred, holding him prisoner with those big brown eyes. 'And move on?'

His heart melted, a lump forming in his throat.

'Guess there's only one way to find out.' Then he kissed her.

'Can I be your best man at the wedding, partner?'

The pair of turtle doves smiled at each other. There was only one answer to that. 'We'd both be honoured,' replied Ruth. Her lips parted as she reached up for more of the same.